"I INVITED YOU INTO MY HOME."

Buffy went on, needing to express her hurt, feeling again her shock and despair. "And then you attacked my family."

"Why not?" he asked almost offhandedly, but his expression was filled with pain. "I killed mine."

He started closing in on her.

"I killed their friends. And their friends' children. For a hundred years I offered an ugly death to everyone I met. And I did it with a song in my heart."

She detected the merest hint of self-loathing; she raised her chin slightly and asked, "What changed?"

"Fed on a girl," he told her. "About your age. Beautiful." He looked off into the distance for a moment. "Dumb as a post. But a favorite among her clan."

"Her clan?" Buffy repeated, unsure of his word choice.

"Romani," he explained. "Gypsics. The elders conjured the perfect punishment for me." He waited a beat. "They restored my soul."

Buffy the Vampire Slayer™

Available from ARCHWAY Paperbacks and POCKET PULSE

Buffy the Vampire Slayer adult books

Available from POCKET BOOKS

BUFFY
THE VAMPIRE
SLAYER™

THE ANGEL CHRONICLES
volume
1

A novelization by Nancy Holder
Based on the screenplays "Angel" and "Reptile Boy"
written by David Greenwalt and "Lie to Me"
written by Joss Whedon

Based on the hit TV series created by Joss Whedon

POCKET PULSE
New York   London   Toronto   Sydney   Singapore

An *Original* Publication of POCKET BOOKS

 POCKET PULSE, published by
Pocket Books, a division of Simon & Schuster, Inc.
1230 Avenue of the Americas, New York, NY 10020

™ and copyright © 1998 by Twentieth Century Fox Film Corporation. All Rights Reserved.

ISBN: 0-671-02133-8

First Pocket Pulse printing July 1998

15 14 13 12 11 10 9

POCKET PULSE and colophon are registered trademarks of Simon & Schuster, Inc.

Printed in the U.S.A.

IL: 9+

For the Slayer and her vampire:
Ms. Sarah Michelle Gellar and Mr. David Boreanaz.

And for my dear friend Christopher Golden,
without whom this book could not have been written,
even though it was.

For the wonderful experience of writing this novelization, I would like to thank: Mr. Joss Whedon and everyone at the *Buffy* production offices, the cast, and the crew; my editor, Lisa Clancy, and her assistant, Elizabeth Shiflett; my terrific agent, Howard Morhaim, and his assistants, Kate Hengerer and Lindsay Sagnette. Thanks also to my dearest husband, Wayne, and to Ida Khabazian and my niece, Rebekah Simpson.

THE ANGEL CHRONICLES

THE CHRONICLES

It was over.

The last two surviving vampires burst out of the Sunnydale club known as the Bronze and fled down the alley, terror on their faces.

Amazed, Angel stepped from the shadows into the moonlight and watched them go. "She did it. I'll be damned."

That beautiful young Slayer had thwarted the Harvest. The threat was over . . . for now.

But the vampires would be back, in full force. Their leader, the Master, imprisoned beneath the earth in a ruined church, would throw everything at the girl until he claimed victory . . . and she died. On that night all the demons, vampires, and other dark forces who walked the night would dance with glee on her grave.

But if he, Angel, believed the Slayer was doomed,

why had he followed her that first night, on her way to the Bronze? To warn her of what was to come? Why had he sought her out, to warn her yet again?

Why was he thinking of her now, and every other waking moment?

He smiled—a slight, almost cold smile—for Angelus, once the scourge of Europe, could never fully let go of his remorse over the terrible evils he had committed. Or of the hatred for what he had once been: the most ruthless vampire who ever hunted down human beings and reveled in their destruction.

Yet recalling his first meeting with Buffy Summers, the Vampire Slayer, he could smile a little.

It was the night he had given her the cross.

As she walked to the local hangout, the Bronze, she had known he was trailing her. Any Slayer would have. And while it was true that she'd caught him by surprise, launching herself down from an overhanging pipe as he turned into the alley to follow her, that was also what he should have expected from the Chosen One.

But he hadn't been prepared for her wit or her beauty. She played with words; she was sarcastic. And yet she grasped both the wonder and the burden of her life as the Slayer.

And, truth be told, he had liked looking into her face when it mirrored her fascination with him. He was used to being admired by women—did the Watcher Diaries not record his full name as "Angelus, the one with the angelic face"? But he was not used to anyone looking past that face into his soul.

His poor soul.

He had not been ready to tell her everything, just to join forces. "I want the same thing you do," he had told her. "To kill them. To kill them all."

Then he had tossed her the jewelry box containing the cross—which he dare not touch himself—and said, of the Harvest, "Don't turn your back on this. You've got to be ready."

But was *he* ready? Angel wondered, recalling their second meeting earlier this very day. She had been going down to the vampires' lair to save a friend. He had shadowed her, wanting to help her, not daring to reveal his true self yet. The timing still wasn't quite right.

He had risked much by telling her his name. Her teacher and Watcher, Rupert Giles, was known and respected as a thorough researcher. *If Giles has all the Watcher Diaries . . .*

Angel wasn't sure he would ever tell her *what* he was. He was already beginning to like her.

Very much.

She would run shrieking from him if she ever learned his secret.

Or else she would kill him.

But because tonight was the Harvest, he had tried to talk her out of going below ground to save a mortal boy.

Her face had been set with determination. "I've got a friend down there—or, a potential friend." She half-smiled. "Do you know what it's like to have a friend?"

He had not smiled back at her question. Perhaps then she had realized that he was friendless and alone. Perhaps she had read the hunger in his face for the things he had abandoned and the things that had been stolen from him.

Perhaps she, too, felt the first stirrings of a longing that should never be acted upon.

But as the vampires fled from the Bronze, their monstrous faces frozen in terror, Angel did smile.

Then he silently moved through the night.

Alone.

Inside the Bronze, Buffy stood with her new Watcher, Rupert Giles, and her two new best friends, Willow Rosenberg and Xander Harris. The ashes of the dead vampires, including the Master's Vessel, were already dissipating in the club's air. Broken furniture was all that remained to mark the vampires' attack.

That, and a few dead bodies of the victims. Most of the patrons had fled, but some remained, stunned and silent.

Buffy noted the carnage. She observed the frightened faces of those she must lay down her life to protect, if need be. She absorbed the brutal fact that she could not escape her fate. Even with her and her mom's move to this new town, Sunnydale, she was, and always would be, the Slayer.

It made her feel set apart. Different.

And in desperate need of someone who understood the darkness she must walk in.

She thought of the intriguing, strikingly handsome young man who seemed intent on helping her. The mysterious Angel.

She wondered if she would ever see him again.

And if she did, what he would be to her, and she to him.

THE FIRST CHRONICLE:

Angel

PROLOGUE

The lair of the undead: a ruined church deep within the earth, stinking of decay, corruption, and death. The deceivingly warm glow of a hundred candles. A pool of blood.

A little boy dropped pebbles into the thick, crimson liquid.

At his side sat a vampire in a leather suit smiling indulgently, his outstretched hand filled with stones for the boy's innocent game.

But this was no ordinary boy. In mortal life, he had been Collin. But then he died. Now he was the Anointed One, and he served the vampire who lounged like a king beside him in an ornately carved chair: the Master, lord of all the vampires on the Hellmouth. In mortal life, the Master had been exactly what he was in death: a monster.

And there was nothing innocent about his game.

Darla approached, returning from her hunting. Like Collin, she was cloaked in innocence: a pretty face framed by blond hair, wearing the uniform of a private girl's school. She practically skipped through the chamber, knowing she was the Master's favorite. With all her icy, heartless, soulless being, she dreamed of the night when the Master would free himself from this dungeon and rule a world filled with vampires, demons, and monsters.

And hopefully, there would be someone else to share the glorious moment with her. Someone with whom she had terrorized Europe. Someone who tore out the throats of the victims she had held down.

His name was on her lips, always.

With his back to her the Master said, "Zackery didn't return from the hunt last night."

Darla came to a stop and hissed, "The Slayer."

The Master's voice was strained but calm. "Zackery was strong, and he was careful. And still the Slayer takes him, as she has taken so many of my family." He took a deep breath and lifted his chin very slightly. "It wears thin." He turned to the Anointed One. "Collin, what would you do about it?"

The Anointed One replied simply in his unworldly voice, "I'd annihilate her."

The Master inhaled with pleasure. "Out of the mouths of babes . . ."

Darla stepped forward eagerly. "Let me do it, Master," she breathed. "Let me kill her for you."

The Master said almost sternly, as if the subject

were distasteful to him, "You have a personal interest in this."

She pouted, "I never get to have *any* fun."

The Master continued in his calm singsong voice, the tone he took when he was at his most dangerous. "I will send the Three."

Darla's eyes filled with excitement. "The Three." Her voice was tinged with anticipation. And pleasure.

And triumph.

CHAPTER 1

He clutched in his fist an ornate silver lighter decorated with a skull and crossbones. The flame flared; he lit the last of three cigarettes, one for each of them.

He and his homies were bad to the bone, and they knew it. Gangbangers. The three of them hung out on a deserted Sunnydale street corner, guarding their turf and eager for action.

Suddenly from around the corner three dark shapes clomped toward them. Their weird body armor gleamed in the dull light. They walked mean.

The three gangbangers straightened up, ready for trouble. Then the three invaders strode into the direct glare of the streetlight, moving fast, ignoring the gangbangers as if they did not exist.

Their faces were hideous. Evil.

13

The gangbangers held their ground for about two seconds, then broke and ran.

The Three kept going, heading down the street.

They *owned* the street.

A cockroach skittered across the floor of the Bronze. A foot zeroed in on it as someone urged in an amused voice, "Get it."

"I got it," a girl announced, and lifted the dead roach off the floor like a trophy. She plopped it into a plastic container on a passing waiter's tray that was half-full with its deceased insectoid brethren and said, "Free drink, please." The waiter, in a silvery T-shirt, nodded happily at her.

Against a backdrop of a banner that read, "FUMIGATION PARTY. *Find a cockroach, get a free drink,"* Willow Rosenberg sat across from Buffy, who in turn sat with her eyes downcast. Buffy had on a cool black crocheted top and wore her blond hair loose with those wispy bang things Willow could not master. Buffy was definitely hotter looking than she was, Willow decided. Her reddish brown hair was just *there,* and her boring, Rosenberg-brown sweater, which her mother had managed to locate for her among all the trendier clothes at the store.

Willow said wryly, "Ah, the fumigation party."

Buffy kept fiddling, but she stirred enough to say, "Hmm?"

"It's an annual tradition," Willow went on. "The closing of the Bronze for a few days to nuke the cockroaches."

"Oh."

Willow persisted. "It's a lot of fun." She smiled kindly at her very glum buddy and said, "What's it like where you are?"

Buffy looked up and laughed, embarrassed. "I'm sorry. I was just thinking about . . . *things.*"

Willow understood at once. "So we're talking about a guy?"

Buffy grimaced and laughed shortly. "Not exactly. For us to have a conversation about a guy there would have to be a guy for us to have a conversation about." She wrinkled her nose. "Was that a sentence?"

Willow said, "You lack a guy."

Sighing, Buffy moved her head. "I do. Which is fine with me most of the time but—"

"What about Angel?"

Buffy made a little face. "Angel? I can just see him in a relationship." She lowered her voice, guy-like: "Hi, honey, you're in grave danger. I'll see you next month."

Willow was sorry. She'd figured the moping was over Buffy's strange but very good-looking sort-of-friend and warning person. *So much for trying to cheer her up.* Nobody could figure out who he was or why he showed up every once in a while to tell Buffy about some new threat to either her existence or that of the entire human race and then disappeared. He knew she was the Slayer, but he didn't offer any information about himself in return. He was incredibly handsome, though. And intense. Very intense.

Sympathetically, she offered, "He's not around much, it's true."

Buffy couldn't seem to stop the smile that crossed her face. She looked radiant as she said, "When he's around, it's like the lights dim everywhere else. You know how it's like that with some guys?"

Willow said, "Oh, yeah."

She gazed at the dance floor where Xander Harris was grooving, his dark, curly hair boyishly hanging in his eyes. He was practically doing aerobics, goofing in a way that Willow understood all too well: *I'm so into my nerdhood you cannot mock me for it.* But Xander was not nerdy. Just underappreciated and undervalued. He didn't realize it. But she did.

She *so* did.

Xander kept on pumping his arms, promoting his night fever routine as Annie Vega glanced his way. He said cheerily, "Hey, Annie," and then when her Neanderthal boyfriend glared at him, added, "Vito! Just leaving."

He swam off in another direction and collided with that foxy landshark known as Cordelia Chase.

"Ouch!" Cordelia cried. She was wearing some kind of low-cut lizard-girl dress and her hair was down, dark and very straight. The Cher of Sunnydale High. "Please keep your extreme oafishness off my two-hundred-dollar shoes."

Man the lifeboats, Xander thought, and said, "Sorry. I was just—"

"Getting off the floor before Annie Vega's boyfriend squashes you like a bug?"

Xander grinned proudly. "Oh, so you noticed."

"Uh-huh."

"Well, thanks for being so understanding."

She flashed him her haughty evil-eye and said, "Sure."

"And I don't know what everyone's talking about," he added in a friendly tone. Then he lobbed the grenade. "That outfit doesn't make you look like a hooker."

If you can't join 'em, psych 'em out—or die trying.

He left the floor while he was maybe ahead, and caught up with his two main gals, Buffy and Willow, who both looked like they were having as much fun as was humanly possible if they were dead.

"Boy, that Cordelia's a regular breath of vile air," he said. When they didn't respond, he cocked his head and said, "What are you vixens up to?"

Willow said, "Just sitting here watching our barren lives pass us by. Oh, look, a cockroach."

Whomp! The sucker didn't have a chance. Xander was about to congratulate her on her technique when he saw not a flicker of predatory satisfaction on her face. Buffy looked even worse.

"Whoa, stop this crazy whirligig of fun," he drawled. "I'm dizzy."

Buffy activated. She said, "All right, now I'm infecting those near and dear to me. I'll see you guys tomorrow." She prepared for liftoff.

Willow said, "Oh, don't go."

Xander piped up, "Yeah, it's early! We could, um, dance." He broke into his standard disco routine.

"Rain check," Buffy said, pushing away from the

table. Smiling, however. Although sadly. To both Slayerettes, she said, " 'Night."

She left. Willow showed Xander the carcass of her kill, attractively glued to her shoe with its cockroachy guts, and said, "Want a free drink?"

Surrounded by people and noise, Angel stood alone as he watched Buffy heading for the Bronze's exit door. He stood in shadow, his face clouded with longing and worry.

Almost as if she sensed him, Buffy looked up.

But he was gone by then.

She moved on.

The street was deserted of people as Buffy headed for home. In the distance an ambulance siren wailed; car horns sounded. Yet, beneath the traffic din, she heard a noise. She slowed and looked back. There was nothing there, but often there seemed to be nothing there while some demon stalked her.

She walked on.

As she half-expected, she heard another sound. She took a few more steps, then stopped. This time she didn't turn around as she said, with resignation and determination in her voice, "It's late. I'm tired and I don't want to play games. Show yourself."

Something dropped to the ground behind her, savagely growling as she whipped a stake out of her jacket and whirled around. As she raised the stake high to strike, a hand grabbed her wrist from behind. A hand with talons for fingernails. It was joined by the hand of another, which yanked her arm. The first twisted her wrist until the stake clattered to the cement.

There were three of them, dressed in weird armor, uncommonly strong, even for vampires.

Buffy said, "Oh, okay nice. Hey, ow, okay. I'm letting go. I don't want to fight all three of you."

Without warning, she kicked the vampire in front of her—he wore a braided ponytail and a wicked-ugly set of fangs—right where it counted. "Unless I have to," she said, and they were off. As the ponytail guy doubled over, another one, who had a scar that had sealed his eye shut, slammed her in the back.

They flung her against a chain link fence. Then two pulled her between them as One-Eye moved in for the kill. He bared his fangs and lowered his face toward her neck. She smelled death on him.

Her death.

Suddenly a familiar voice rang out as someone yanked One-Eye's head back.

Angel.

He said, "Good dogs don't bite."

Buffy threw herself backward, kicking her legs up and catching her two captors in the head. One went down. Ponytail grabbed her and threw her against the fence as Angel dodged One-Eye.

Angel moved like a panther: fast, savage, and deadly. He went for the one who had fallen as One-Eye ripped a pointed spike off the wrought iron fence and lunged at him.

"Look out!" Buffy shouted as he slashed Angel across the ribs. She fought Ponytail, smashing his head back with her open hands, and then slamming both her fists, doubled together like a wrecking ball, into his face.

Angel was down; she paused to kick One-Eye in the face, then urged Angel to his feet, screaming, "Run!"

They flew. Down one block, through an empty lot, and across another block as they moved into a residential area. Angel matched her step for step, almost as if he knew where she was leading them. As one, they turned onto Revello Drive. Buffy spared a glance at him; he was holding his side. She frowned, worried, but pumped harder as the snarling vampires gained on them. Dashing ahead of Angel she opened the front door.

She herded him inside, yelling, "Get in! Come on!"

Just as she shut the door, One-Eye leaped onto the porch, grabbing for her. She smashed his hand with the door. He pulled it free and she slammed the door shut. She locked it as she looked through the panes, fighting to catch her breath.

Behind her, Angel said, "It's all right. A vampire can't come in unless it's invited."

"I've heard that before, but I've never put it to the test."

The three vampires paced the porch, growling. She didn't know how long they would loiter, but it appeared Angel was right. They weren't going to be able to come in without an invitation. A comfort, that.

As was the sight of Angel standing in her house,

hurt, but alive and staring back at her with his dark, penetrating eyes.

She said, "I'll get some bandages. Take your jacket and your shirt off."

He followed her into the kitchen, shedding his black jacket and pulling his white T-shirt over his head. She reached to get the first aid kit out of the cupboard.

Then as she turned and saw that he had his back to her and was naked from the waist up, her heart began to pound. She paused, hypnotized by the sleek taper of the muscles in his back and his arms, the smooth skin on the nape of his neck.

A large tattoo of a flying creature rippled on his right shoulder as he moved slightly, and she stirred from her daze and said, "Nice tattoo."

Then she began to bandage his wound. He was cold. That made sense; he was shirtless and it was chilly out. His wound was deep, and she was surprised that he didn't seem to be in more pain.

They were standing very close together. Buffy was aware that his face—his lips—were inches from hers. To distract herself, she said, "I was lucky you came along." Then, regaining her composure to a degree, she tilted her head up at him and asked with a tinge of mock suspicion, "How *did* you happen to come along?"

He replied, his voice soft and deep, "I live nearby. I was just out walking."

"So you weren't following me? I had this feeling you were."

21

His smile was faint, but it was there. "Why would I do that?"

She spoke rapidly, her fingers ripping through the sterile packaging in the kit. "You tell me. You're the Mystery Guy who appears out of nowhere." She gave a little laugh. "I'm not saying I'm not happy about it tonight, but if you *are* hanging around me, I'd like to know why."

She finished the bandage and straightened up, now even closer to him.

He said, "Maybe I like you."

She stared up at him, catching the scent of his body, the light sweat, the smell of soap or maybe incense. "Maybe?" she asked, somewhere between hopeful and playful.

He made no answer, only gazed at her. Buffy took a breath. She just knew that something was going to happen.

Something did happen.

The front door opened.

Yikes!

Buffy raced to the door. Her mother was still standing on the porch, putting her keys back in her purse and reaching to open the mailbox. Buffy jerked her mother inside and scanned for the enemy.

Joyce Summers said, "Honey, what are you doing?"

After glancing out at the yard, Buffy quickly closed and locked the door. "There's a lot of weird people out at night, and I just feel better with you safe and sound inside."

Then her next thought was of the handsome,

older, shirtless guy in their kitchen and she said frantically, "You must be beat!"

Her mother did look weary. She nodded. "I am. For a little gallery, you have no idea how much—"

Buffy cut in, eager to move her along. "Why don't you go upstairs and get into bed, and I can bring you some hot tea."

Joyce looked pleasantly surprised. "That's sweet. What did you do?"

It took Buffy a moment to register the question. Still pushing for innocence, she made her eyes wide. "Can't a daughter just be concerned about her mother?"

Joyce's gaze ticked past her. She said, "Hi."

Behind Buffy, Angel answered, "Hi."

Uh-oh. The jig was up. Luckily Angel had slipped back into his clothes. Buffy blathered, "Uh, okay. Um, Angel, this is my mom. Mom, this is Angel. We ran into each other on the way home." *And if she believes that one, I have some doctored report cards she could sign. . . .*

Angel said, "Hello. Nice to meet you."

"What do you do, Angel?" her mother asked, very politely squaring off as Angel hesitated: older guy versus dateable girl's parent. Round one.

Buffy covered for him, saying, "He's a student." She realized he looked a little too old to be in high school. "First year community college. Angel's been helping me with my history." She laughed. "You know I've been toiling there."

It was unclear how much, if any, of that her

mother believed. Her mom said, "It's a little late for tutoring. I'm going to go to bed, and . . . Buffy?"

Hint, hint.

"I'll say good night and do the same," Buffy promised.

Her mother gave Angel another scrutinizing once-over. "It was nice to meet you."

She headed upstairs.

The Slayer held the front door to her home open and called loudly, "Good night. We'll hook up soon and do that study thing."

She shut the door and motioned to the waiting Angel to go upstairs with her. He followed her, aware of her closeness, aware that they were going to her bedroom.

He slipped inside as she checked down the hall, then shut her door. Quietly he said, "Look, I don't want to get you in any more trouble."

"And I don't want to get you dead," she insisted. "They could still be out there. So, uh. Oh." She looked around, almost as if she had never been in her own room before. "Two of us," she said awkwardly. "One bed. That doesn't work. Um, why don't you take the bed? You know, because you're wounded."

Angel was touched by her concern. Her hands on his body had been gentle and careful; he thought of them now as he said firmly, "I'll take the floor." To cut off her protest, he added, "Oh, believe me, I've had worse."

"Okay." She gestured toward the window. "Then,

ah, why don't you see if the Fang Gang is loitering and, um, keep your back turned while I change."

Angel smiled and crossed to the window, dutifully turning his back. He could hear the rustle of clothing as he studied the black night. Nothing moved outside, as if all was serene.

"I don't see them," he reported.

Inside, Buffy's bedroom was not serene. It pulsed with tension and excitement. His. And hers, too. Of that he was certain.

"You know, I'm the Chosen One," she said. He kept his back turned, unsure if she was finished dressing. "It's my job to fight guys like that. What's your excuse?"

"Somebody has to," he murmured.

"Well, what does your family think of your career choice?"

How far should I go? What do I tell her? He replied simply, "They're dead."

Buffy stopped and turned toward him. The moonlight streaming through the window blinds cast shadows across his face almost like bars. His profile was sharply chiseled, and with her gaze, Buffy traced the silhouette. She asked quietly, "Was it vampires?"

He turned toward her, his face filled with unspoken pain.

"It was."

"I'm sorry."

"It was a long time ago." His voice betrayed buried sorrow, hidden anger.

"So this is a vengeance gig for you?" she pressed.

For a moment there was silence. Then he looked at her, really looked, and said, "You even look pretty when you go to sleep."

Suddenly she wished she had changed into more than her T-shirt and pajama bottoms. She smiled weakly and said, "Well, when I wake up, it's an entirely different story. Here." She handed him a quilt and a pillow. "Sleep tight."

In the moonlit stillness they lay, she on her bed, he on the floor. Both awake, both staring at the ceiling, each acutely aware of the presence of the other. They had faced death together, and now they faced the nearness of each other.

"Angel?" Buffy whispered.

"Hmmm?"

"Do you snore?"

He smiled, just a little. "I don't know. It's been a long time since anybody's been in a position to let me know."

Buffy's smile was bigger than his. *A long time since.* That was good. That was a thought she could drift away on, sleep and dream on.

But Angel stayed awake all night, listening to the beating of her heart.

CHAPTER 2

The next day, in what doubled as Slayage World Headquarters the Sunnydale High School library—Buffy told Xander, Willow, and Giles what had happened the night before.

"He spent the *night?* In your room? In your bed?" Xander almost shouted.

Buffy flushed at her friend's outrage. "Not *in* my bed. *By* my bed."

"That is so romantic," Willow said dreamily. No outrage there. A little envy, maybe. "Wow. Did you, uh, I mean did he, uh—"

Buffy said proudly, "Perfect gentleman."

"Oh, Buffy, come on! Wake up and smell the seduction." Xander frowned big time. "It's the oldest trick in the book."

Buffy asked pointedly, "Saving my life? Getting slashed in the ribs?"

27

"Du-uh. Guys'll do anything to impress a girl." Xander pushed out his chest. "I once drank an entire gallon of Gatorade without taking a breath."

Willow nodded, backing him up. "It was pretty impressive." Then she made a little face. "Although later there was an *ick* factor. . . ."

Giles approached, carrying a huge black leather-bound book. "Can we steer this riveting conversation back to the events that took place earlier in the evening? You left the Bronze and were set upon by three unusually virile vampires . . ."

Giles laid down the book and pointed to an engraving. "Did they look like this?"

They were Buffy's three vampire amigos.

Buffy nodded. "Yeah. What's with the uniforms?"

Giles looked grim but satisfied. That happened whenever he was right about some ravening monster intent upon either sucking Buffy's liver out through her nose or causing the basic end of the world as it was known and loved. "It seems you encountered the Three—warrior vampires, very proud and strong."

Willow blinked, impressed. "How is it you always know this stuff? You always know what's going on. I never know what's going on."

Giles waved a hand at the piles of dusty books as he sipped from a coffee cup. "Well, you weren't here from midnight to six researching it." Buffy's call had reached him just as he was ready to turn in.

Sheepishly Willow agreed. "No, I was sleeping."

Giles turned to Buffy. "Obviously, you're hurting the Master. He wouldn't send the Three for just anyone." He thought a moment, cleaning his glasses. "We must step up our training with weapons."

Xander added, "Buffy, you'd better stay at my place until these samurai guys are history."

Buffy wasn't quite sure she'd heard him right. "What?"

"Don't worry about Angel," he went on. "Willow can run over to your house and tell him to get out of town fast."

Giles shook his head. "Angel and Buffy are not in immediate jeopardy." He put his glasses back on. "Eventually the Master will send someone else, but in the meantime, the Three, having failed, will offer up their own lives as penance."

Buffy nodded to herself, a little tired, a little wigged. *Three down, how many more bazillions left to go?*

Deep within the earth, the Three knelt before the Master. They still carried their aura of menace and destruction, yet they were afraid. Darla watched with excitement as they hung their heads in shame. The leader of the Three, so scarred that one eye was permanently shut, handed the Master a long, sharp impaling spear—a vampiric weapon of execution. Acting as if he had no plans to use it, the Master handed it in turn to Darla, who clutched it eagerly.

Their leader said, "We failed in our duty, and now our lives belong to you."

The Master moved to Collin, and spoke gently in his dangerously warm voice. "Pay attention, child. You are the Anointed One, and there is much you must learn. With power comes responsibility. True, they did fail, but also true, we who walk at night share a common bond. The taking of a life—I'm not talking about humans, of course—is a serious matter."

The leader of the Three raised his head slightly. Darla knew he was hoping that he and the others would be allowed to live.

Sounding like the little human boy he once had been, Collin asked, "So you would spare them?"

The Master gave Darla a look. They had been together so long, killed so many, that she understood what he wanted. Her eyes shining, she clamped her hands around the impaling spear and quietly took her position behind the leader of the Three.

"I am weary," the Master said, "and their deaths will bring me little joy." He shepherded Collin off a little way.

It was Darla's cue. With all her strength and her pent-up rage, she gleefully shoved the spear through the scarred, powerful vampire. He shrieked, and then exploded into dust.

The shrieks of his brothers followed quickly.

"Of course," the Master added, "sometimes a little is enough."

The library door was half covered with a large sign that read, Closed for filing. Please come back tomorrow.

The sign seemed to Buffy an unnecessary precaution. As did Giles's sweep of the hall to make sure it was clear, the locking of the doors, yada yada yada. Nobody at Sunnydale High was into the book-checking-out thing. More like the guy-and-girl-checking-out thing. And if you had an ounce of coolness, you did not go hunting for acceptable date material in the school library. She shook her head.

Buffy peered into a large locker filled with weaponry. Some girls got to spend their afternoons picking out slip dresses, and some girls got to try machetes on for size.

"Cool, a crossbow," she said as she touched the ancient weapon. Then she saw the arrows—*more correctly, the bolts. Hey, witness knowledge girl!*—and started to load the weapon. "Huh, check out these babies," she purred. "Goodbye stakes, hello flying fatality." Eagerly, she looked around. "What can I shoot?"

Looking perturbed with her—a frequent occupational hazard for this Slayer—Giles, in padded gear, took the crossbow and put it away, saying firmly, "Nothing. The crossbow comes later. You must first become proficient with the basic tools of combat. Let's begin with the quarter staff." He plucked up two long wooden poles and handed one to her. "Which, incidentally, will require countless hours of rigorous training. I speak from experience."

She looked at the pole, then at him, and almost cracked up. "Giles, twentieth century?" she said. "I'm not going to be fighting Friar Tuck."

Cracking up was the farthest thing from his mind. He replied with all his British-accented seriousness,

"You never know with whom—or what—you may be fighting." He put on a padded helmet. "And these traditions have been handed down through the ages." He picked up the quarter staff. "Now you show me good, steady progress with the quarter staff, and in due time we'll discuss the crossbow."

He held the quarter staff across his body with both hands and got ready to rumble, Giles-style. "Now, put on your pads," he told her.

She cocked her head. "I'm not going to need pads for you."

He accepted her challenge with a slight lift of his chin. "We'll see about that." He saluted her by raising the right end of the staff. *"En garde."*

Her first thrust was a bit tentative and he parried it easily; then, as wood smacked wood, she got the feel of the rhythm and fell immediately into it: thrust, parry, thrust, parry, thrust, thrust, thrust. She hit him high, low, in the middle, *wham!* practically heard his bones crack. He had taught her not to hold back; part of his duty as Watcher was to give her a real fight.

Whack! She knocked him flat on his back. Breathing hard, he stared up at her and wheezed, "Good. Let's move on to the crossbow."

Good. Let's move on to Angel, Buffy thought, as she carried the plastic bag of dinner leftovers upstairs. Her heart was pounding. While she had gone through the paces of her life, he had been waiting in her house all day. At least she hoped he was still there. Between training with Giles, catching a ride home with her mom and being roped into kitchen duty, she hadn't gotten a chance to sneak upstairs and check on him.

Taking a breath, she opened her bedroom door, slipped in, and shut the door behind herself.

"Angel?"

"Hey," he said. He stepped from the shadows as if he had blended into them, as if they were some kind of protective coloring.

She held up the plastic bag and said, "Brought you some dinner." He looked curiously at the bag, then back up at her face. "It's a little plateless, sorry. So. What'd you do all day?"

"I read a little." He gestured toward her dresser. "And just thought about a lot of things." His face was deadly serious. "Buffy, I—"

She was looking in the direction he had pointed. The dresser. Her diary lay on the top of the dresser. As she registered its presence, her mouth dropped open in horror. "My diary?" she squeaked. "You read my diary?"

She marched to the dresser, put the diary in the top drawer, and slammed it shut.

"That is *not* okay. A diary is a person's most private place and you don't even know what I was writing about. *Hunk* can mean a lot of things, bad things, and where it says your eyes are 'penetrating' I meant to write 'bulgy'—"

"Buffy, I—" he said, stepping toward her.

"And *A* doesn't stand for Angel, for that matter.

33

It stands for . . . Achmed, a charming foreign exchange student, and so that whole fantasy part has nothing to do with you at all—"

Angel cut in. "Your mother moved your diary when she came in to straighten up. I watched her from the closet. I didn't read it, I swear."

"Oh." She took that in. Diary: still private.

Then she realized how she'd babbled on about all the good parts in the diary just like some babbling brook thingie. Damage: worse than if he had read it.

"Ohhhhh." Where were those trap doors when you needed to be swallowed up?

He didn't seem to notice her acute humiliation. He was focused on something else. Something more intense to him. "I did a lot of thinking today," he began. "I can't really be around you."

Oh, no. She shrugged to show she wasn't dying inside. "Hey, no big."

"Because when I am—"

"Water over . . . the bridge—" *Wait. That wasn't right . . .*

"All I can think about is how badly I want to kiss you," he continued, but it didn't register with her at first.

She pressed on resolutely, determined not to let him see how very much she so did not want him to leave her life: "It's *under* the bridge, *over* the dam . . ." and then she heard what he had said. "Kiss me?" she echoed, looking up at him.

His face lost none of its seriousness. He was finding no joy in telling her this. "I'm older than you, and this can't ever . . ." He stopped, then seemed to surrender to something. "I should go."

She asked softly, "How . . . how much older?"

Again he hesitated. He looked deeply into her eyes. A rush of warmth shot through her; head to toes, she tingled. Her face was hot. Her hands were cold.

"I should . . ."

"Go, you said." She moved toward him, knowing that he wasn't going. Knowing, with a thrill, that he couldn't make himself leave.

She lifted her chin; he cradled it with his fingers. Then his lips were on hers. It was the softest kiss; tender, unsure.

Angel, Angel, Buffy sang inside. Everything else fell away: being the Slayer and being sixteen and being anything or anywhere but in Angel's arms, and kissing Angel's mouth.

They both tensed as the kiss became more passionate. *Yes.* She gave herself to the moment, held tightly in his arms as she kissed him fiercely and he kissed her back with increasing intensity. His hand gripped her arms, pulling her closer, then . . . She realized he was struggling against her, trying to push himself free.

He backed away and averted his face.

"What?" she asked, panting a little. "Angel, what's wrong?"

Suddenly, he looked at her. The dark eyes were wild and blank, like an animal's. His soft mouth was pulled back, revealing sharp, pointed teeth . . .

Fangs.

BUFFY, THE VAMPIRE SLAYER

She screamed in terror.

Snarling, Angel dove out the window. He rolled down the roof, hit the ground, and raced into the night as Buffy kept screaming.

No. No. No.

The door to her bedroom burst open. Her mother ran in, calling, "Buffy, what happened?"

Buffy fought to catch her breath. She could say nothing. How to explain? Where to begin?

She must deal with this alone. But she was in such shock. Such pain . . .

"Nothing," she managed. "I saw a shadow."

CHAPTER 3

"**A**ngel's a vampire?" Willow's stunned reaction mirrored Buffy's own.

The light of day hadn't diminished the shock as she was sharing Angel's terrible secret with the Scooby Gang at school the next morning.

Buffy felt sick. "I can't believe this is happening. One minute we're kissing, the next minute . . ." She turned to Giles, almost begging when she asked, "Can a vampire ever be a good person? Couldn't it happen?"

Though Giles could be the soul of tact, he had never actually lied to her. At least, not that she knew of. *This could be the one time and I would be totally cool with that,* she thought as he started the words she dreaded hearing.

"A vampire isn't a person at all. It may have the movements, the memories, even the personality of the person it took over. But it is a demon at the core. There's no halfway."

Willow looked at Buffy. "So that'd be a no, huh?"

Buffy couldn't believe it. "Well, then, what was he doing? Why was he . . . good to me? Was it all some part of the Master's plan? It doesn't make sense." *Besides, it's too horrible to be true.*

Bone weary, soul wounded, Buffy sat with Willow on one of the benches in front of the school. Xander, silent up to now, sat down next to her, grasping his skateboard.

"All right, you have a problem and it's not a small one," he began. "Let's just take a breath and look at this calmly and objectively."

Buffy half-nodded. He was making sense. She waited, with hope, for the solution to her problem.

And Xander handed it to her: "Angel's a vampire, you're a Slayer. I think it's obvious what you have to do."

No, she thought desperately. She looked to Giles.

Giles sighed. "It *is* the Slayer's duty."

Xander continued. "I know you have feelings for this guy, but it's not like you're in love with him, right?"

Buffy said nothing, but Xander must have read the answer on her face. He blew up. "You're in love with a vampire?" he said loudly. "What, are you out of your mind?"

"What!"

Standing directly behind him, Cordelia Chase reacted with shock.

Xander looked stricken. "Not *vampire*." He said

sternly to Buffy, "How can you love an *umpire?* Everyone hates them!"

Cordelia's nostrils flared like those of a bull ready to charge. Delicately, however. "Where did you get that dress?" she demanded.

Buffy and the others watched as the cheerleader zeroed in on another girl crossing the quad in the exact same dress as Cordelia's, black with a colorful pop-art design. Cordelia snapped, "This is a one-of-a-kind Todd Oldham. Do you know how much this dress cost?"

The girl tried to scoot away, but Cordelia was having none of it. She grabbed the back of the girl's dress and tried to read the label, hissing, "It's a knockoff, isn't it?"

The girl renewed her efforts to escape. The queen of the fashion police gave chase. "It's a cheesy knockoff! This is what happens when you sign these free trade agreements."

The two disappeared into the crowd. Flatly, Buffy quipped, "And we think *we* have problems."

Angel walked down the basement corridor that led to his apartment. The door was unlocked; he entered. The soft light cloaked much of the room in shadow; as he turned on another light, he froze, sensing a presence.

"Who's here?" he demanded, unafraid but alert.

"A friend." He turned to look. It was Darla. He tensed as she emerged from the shadows, smiling, enjoying his unease.

* * *

"Hi," she said. "It's been a while."

Angel replied evenly, "A lifetime."

"Or two. But who's counting?"

He gestured to her clothes. "What's with the Catholic-schoolgirl look? Last time I saw you it was kimonos."

"And last time I saw you, it wasn't high school girls." She could not realize how much that comment hurt him. The look of horror on Buffy's face was burned into his brain. "Don'tcha like?" she asked, making a tiny curtsy. "Remember Budapest, turn of the century? You were such a *bad* boy during that earthquake." She came toward him, moving slowly, almost as if she were preparing for an attack.

The memory of his own evil actions pained him, as did almost every memory he had of his entire vampiric existence. He replied, "You did some damage yourself."

Her chuckle was low and breathy. She was beautiful, for the moment. "Is there anything better than a natural disaster? The panic, the people lost in the streets. Like picking fruit off the vine."

She glided through his apartment, examining his possessions. It was clear she considered him to be a possession of hers.

She looked at his bed. "Nice," she observed ironically. "You're living above ground, like one of them. You and your new friend are attacking us, like one of them. But guess what, precious? You're not one of them—"

Without warning, she yanked a string on a shade

and snapped it open. A beam of sunlight hit Angel like an arc of fire. The pain shot deep into his bones as he shouted and fell to the floor.

"Are you?"

He climbed slowly to his feet and set his jaw, unwilling to allow her to witness his agony. "No, but I'm not exactly one of you, either."

"Is that what you tell yourself these days?" She moved to the fridge and opened the door. Bags of blood hung from the top rack. He knew what she thought of them as she eyed their blood-bank labels contemptuously: this blood was cold, dead, and lifeless. There could not possibly be any sense of rapture or wonder in drinking it.

That was the price he was willing to pay to set himself apart from vampires like Darla. From every other vampire he knew.

"You're not exactly living off quiche," she drawled. She walked toward him again. "You and I both know what you hunger for. What you *need*. Hey, it's nothing to be ashamed of. It's who we are. It's what makes eternal life worth living."

She touched his chest and began to caress it. He did not react, but he was furious. She looked up at him with a suggestive smile. "You can only suppress your real nature for so long. I can feel it brewing inside of you. I hope I'm around when it explodes."

"Maybe you don't want to be," he said in a low, dangerous voice as he glared at her.

"I'm not afraid of you. I bet *she* is, though." She left him and headed for the door. "Or maybe I'm underestimating her. Talk to her. Tell her about the curse. Maybe she'll come around. And if she still doesn't trust you, you know where I'll be."

She sauntered out the door.

Angel stared straight ahead, hating her. Hating the truths she had forced on him. Hating the look of terror he saw on Buffy's lovely face when he had revealed his true self. Sometimes lies were better. Such as the lie he had begun to allow himself to believe: that it mattered that he was sorry down to the very core of the soul for all the terrible acts he had committed. That it made what he had done less unforgivable.

That it made him a man again.

He wondered if Buffy would hunt him now. And if she did, what he would do.

Ah, research. Facts would save this relationship. Of that, Willow was not sure. But she could hope.

In the school library, Willow and Buffy sat at the table while Xander stood to one side. All were looking through books about demons and vampires and all the other ick-factor things Willow had started reading about when Buffy came into her life.

"Here's something at last," Giles announced, emerging from the stacks and shattering the silence.

Xander jumped perhaps a foot. "Can you please warn us before you do that?"

Giles was carrying some very old, weathered-looking books. Ignoring Xander, he continued, "There's nothing about Angel in the texts, but then it occurred to me it's been ages since I read the diaries of any of the Watchers before me."

Willow looked brightly at Buffy. "That must have been so embarrassing when you thought he'd read *your* diary, but then it turned out he felt the same way that—" She caught herself and said to Giles, "I'm listening."

Giles referred to one of the volumes he was holding and said, "There's a mention some two hundred years ago in Ireland of Angelus, the one with the angelic face."

Buffy's expression was ironic. "They got *that* right."

Xander coughed. Everyone looked at him. He put on a innocent expression and said, "I'm not saying anything. I have nothing to say."

Checking the book, Giles went on, "Does Angel have a tattoo behind his right shoulder?"

Buffy nodded. "Yeah. It's a bird or something."

Xander's eyes widened. He leaned forward slightly and said, *"Now* I'm saying something. You saw him *naked?"*

Willow tried to bring the the subject back to safer territory. "So Angel's been around a while."

Giles gave his head a little shake. "Not that long for a vampire. Two hundred and forty years or so."

Buffy gave a little laugh. A gallows laugh. Willow was so sorry for her. "Two hundred and forty. Well, he said he was older."

Oblivious to Buffy's distress, Giles sat down and consulted another diary. "Angelus leaves Ireland, wreaks havoc in Europe for several decades. Then, about eighty years ago, a most curious thing happens . . ." He reached for another book. "He comes to America, shuns other vampires, and lives alone. There's no record of him hunting here."

Willow perked up. She said, "So he *is* a good vampire. I mean, on a scale of one to ten, ten being someone who's killing and maiming every night and one being someone who's . . . not . . ." She flushed at her word choices and the sad expression on Buffy's face.

"I'm sorry," Giles said. "There's no record but, vampires hunt and kill. It's what they do."

"Fish gotta swim, birds gotta fly," Xander quipped, but it wasn't funny.

"He could have fed on me. He didn't," Buffy offered.

"Question," Xander went on. "The hundred years or so before he came to our shores, what was he like then?" Willow didn't know if the edge in his voice came from being protective toward Buffy or jealous of Angel, but it was there.

Giles said plainly, "Like all of them." He looked directly at Buffy, making sure she heard his words. "A vicious, violent animal."

In the Master's lair, Darla faced her demon lord and said, "Don't think I'm not grateful, you letting me kill the Three."

The Master made a sweeping gesture. "How can my children learn if I do everything for them?" He smiled at Collin, the Anointed One, who sat near-by.

"But you've got to let me take care of the Slayer," Darla added. She would like nothing better than to drain every drop of blood from Angel's little human.

The Master raised his brow and said, in his singsong voice, "Oh, you're giving me orders now."

She walked away, saying over her shoulder, "Okay, then we'll just do nothing while she takes us out one by one." Her voice was soft, her words lilting, almost an imitation of the Master.

"Do I sense a plan, Darla?" the Master inquired. She smiled and turned at his invitation. "Share."

She said, "Angel kills her and comes back to the fold."

"Angel," the Master murmured. He looked off into the distance, perhaps seeing the same thing Darla did: Angelus, scourge of Europe, a ravening beast. "He was the most vicious creature I ever met. I miss him."

"So do I." That went without saying.

"Why would he kill her if he feels for her?" the Master asked.

Darla smiled. "To keep her from killing him."

The Master returned her smile and bit his tongue with pleasure. He said to the Anointed One, "You see how we all work together for the common good? That's how a family is supposed to function."

Willow was doing the tutor thing. Buffy was doing the lost-in-thought thing. Call it a study date.

Call Buffy's life bipolar: death and quizzes.

Willow said slowly. "So Reconstruction began when?" She waited. "Buffy?"

Buffy stirred. "Huh? Oh. Reconstruction. Reconstruction began after ah, the construction, which was shoddy, so they had to reconstruct—"

Willow saved her. "After the *destruction* of the Civil War."

Buffy took that in. "Right. The Civil War." She began to drift away again. "During which, Angel was already like . . . a hundred and change."

Willow asked gently, "Are we going to talk about boys or are we going to help you pass history?" She waited a moment, then shut her history book and leaned toward Buffy. They were alone in the library, but she lowered her voice anyway. "Sometimes I have this fantasy that Xander's just going to grab me and kiss me right on the lips."

Buffy warmed to the subject. "You want Xander, you gotta speak up, girl."

Willow looked utterly panicked. "No, no, no! No speaking up. That way leads to madness and sweaty palms."

Above them, behind the stacks on the second floor of the library, Darla listened. The Slayer's young, innocent friend lowered her voice and said, "Okay, here's something I've got to know. When Angel kissed you, I mean, before he turned into . . . how was it?"

The Slayer got all rosy and dreamy. She said,

"Unbelievable." She laughed softly, the way Darla remembered that young girls in love laughed.

Her friend was impressed. "Wow. And it *is* kind of novel how he'll stay young and handsome forever. Although you'll still get wrinkly and die and ooo, what about the children?" She must have realized she was hurting the Slayer, for she said quickly, "I'll be quiet now."

The Slayer cocked her head and smiled sadly. "No, it's okay. I need to hear this. I need to get over him so I can—"

"So that you can . . . ?" The girl mimed a staking with her silly fuzzy-topped pen. Darla felt a thrill of anticipation. Implementing her plan was going to be easier than she had expected.

The Slayer shrugged. "Like Xander said, I'm a Slayer. And he's a vampire. God, I can't. He's never done anything to hurt me." She caught herself. "Okay, now. I've got to stop thinking about this." Resolutely she opened her schoolbook. "Okay. Give me another half hour, and maybe something will sink in. Then I'm going home for some major moping."

"Okay. The era of congressional Reconstruction," the Slayer's friend intoned dutifully, "usually called Radical . . ."

Darla glided away. She had a lot to accomplish in the next half hour.

Joyce Summers faced mounds of paperwork at the kitchen table. She poured herself a cup of coffee and took a sip.

There was a slow, deliberate creaking somewhere in the house. She looked up. Hearing nothing more, she settled back to work on the account books for the gallery.

There it was again. It was outside. She stood, a little spooked, and went to the back door. She peered out the window and saw nothing.

But as the mother of the Slayer turned away, she missed the sight of Darla, her features contorted in her vampiric face, grinning in anticipation of the unfolding of her scheme. Then Darla moved silently from the window.

Joyce continued to move through the house, growing edgier at the creaks and groans. *For heaven's sake! It's just the house settling,* she told herself, but she started, just a little, when someone knocked on the front door.

It was a lovely blond girl with a very sweet smile. She was carrying schoolbooks, and she was very conservatively dressed. As Joyce opened the door, she thought fleetingly that she wished Buffy dressed like this.

"Hello?" Joyce asked politely.

"Hi. I'm Darla. A friend of Buffy's?" the girl said tentatively.

"Oh." Joyce relaxed. "Nice to meet you."

A pause.

"She didn't mention anything about me coming over for a study date, did she?" Darla smiled shyly.

Joyce was a little confused, just the tiniest bit alarmed. "No," she said. "I thought she was studying with Willow at the library." Back in Los Angeles, there had been so many unexplained disappearances. She hoped all that was behind them now.

"She is," Darla assured her. "Willow's the Civil War expert, but then I was supposed to help her with the War of Independence." Her smile became modest and genteel. "My family kind of goes back to those days."

"Well, I know she's supposed to be home soon," Joyce said. "Would you like to come in and wait?"

Darla stepped over the threshold of the Summers home. "Very nice of you to invite me into your home," she said.

Joyce smiled, bemused. It was an odd thing to say, but kids were like that. Sometimes awkward, sometimes charming, sometimes both. She liked this girl. "You're welcome," she said as Darla came in. She added conversationally, "I've been wrestling with the I.R.S. all night. Would you like something to eat?"

Darla said, "Yes. I would."

"Let's see what we have." Joyce led the way to the kitchen, asking over her shoulder. "Do you feel like something little or something big?"

"Something big," Darla replied, allowing her true self—her vampire self—to be revealed. Soon, now, very soon, Angel would be hers.

He couldn't stay away. He *had* to talk to Buffy. Angel walked up to Buffy's front door and raised his hand to knock. He stopped himself and with a sigh walked away. That was what he had to do.

Walk away.

He was almost past the house when someone screamed in terror. He bolted around to the back and flung open the door.

Buffy's mother was slumped in Darla's arms. Blood flowed from twin wounds on her neck. Darla's demon mouth was covered with the woman's blood.

"Let her go."

Darla looked at him and laughed. "I just had a little. There's plenty more. Aren't you hungry for something warm after all this time?"

Angel hesitated, starting to breathe a little harder as he smelled the tantalizing odor of warm, living blood. It was true; he was hungry for it. He was always hungry for it.

Darla spoke in a sexy, inviting voice, holding Joyce Summers like a rag doll. "Come on, Angel."

He shook his head, fighting the change, fighting the need. This was a living human being. This was Buffy's mother.

"Just say yes," Darla breathed, and heaved the unconscious woman into his arms. He struggled with his burden, fighting hard, struggling but feeling himself losing. He was weakening, too hungry, almost starving for it.

He felt his face change. He slipped easily, *too easily,* into vampire mode. Darla's eyes burned with delight as she said triumphantly, "Welcome home."

She moved toward the door, leaving him alone

with Joyce Summers in his grip. Angel stared at the blood on her neck, the fresh, warm blood . . .

He shut his eyes, trying to control himself. He opened them, moving his head—and fangs—down toward Joyce's neck. Darla's bite was shallow. Glistening. Closer . . .

"Hey," a voice called. "I'm home."

Buffy entered from the hallway and froze.

Angel could not speak; the hunger was so fierce upon him. The hunger . . . and the shame.

Throwing Angel through the large window in the front of the Summers house wasn't the neatest way to get rid of him, but Buffy didn't care. *Neatness doesn't always count.* Angel landed in a heap on the lawn. But of course he wasn't hurt; he got to his feet and faced her.

She had never hated anyone as much as she hated him in that moment. She said quietly, dangerously, "You're not welcome here. You come near us and I'll kill you."

He said nothing, only looked at her with his dark, brutal eyes and his hideous face. She turned her back on him and raced into the kitchen, grabbing the phone and dialing 911.

"Mom, Mom, can you hear me?" she asked frantically, and then, into the receiver, "Yes. I need an ambulance at sixteen-thirty Revello Drive. My mother . . . cut herself. She's lost a lot of blood. Please, please hurry." She hung up. "Mom?"

The back door opened. She turned, half-expecting

another attack from Angel. Xander and Willow filed in.

"Hey, Buffy," Xander said, then saw her mother on the floor. "Oh, my God."

Willow gasped. "What happened?"

"Angel," Buffy said, and her world shattered.

CHAPTER 4

Giles strode down the hospital corridor and into Joyce Summers's room. She was resting, a small bandage on her neck. Buffy stood protectively beside her bed, Willow and Xander a slight distance away.

Buffy was saying, "Do you remember anything, Mom?"

Her mother was fuzzy. "Just . . . your friend came over. I was going to make a snack."

Filled with guilt, Buffy echoed, "My friend."

Joyce slurred as she continued, "I guess I slipped and cut my neck on . . ." She paused. "The doctor said it looked like a barbecue fork. We don't *have* a barbecue fork." She inquired of Giles, "Are you another doctor?"

Buffy interjected, "Mom, this is Mr. Giles."

"The librarian from your school?" the poor woman said. "What's he——?"

Giles stepped forward. "I just came to pay my respects. To wish you a speedy recovery."

She took that into her sedative-filled head. "Boy, the teachers really do care in this town."

Buffy said, "Get some rest now." She gave her mother a kiss on the cheek and walked out of the room, her friends following her.

In the corridor, Buffy leaned wearily against the wall. "She's going to be okay. They gave her some iron. Her blood count was a little . . ."

Giles could see her fighting for control. He was deeply moved by her plight. Though she was the Chosen One, the champion of mankind against the powers of Darkness, she was also a sixteen-year-old girl in love with the most inappropriate . . . er, person.

"A little low," he said, giving her time to collect herself. He wished he could do or say something to comfort her, but he must stand as the voice of reason. The only voice, if necessary. It was his duty to protect her, not to give her what she wanted.

He continued, "It presents itself like a mild anemia. You're lucky you got to her as soon as you did."

She whipped her head toward him. "Lucky? Stupid," she said miserably.

"Buff, it's not your fault," Xander insisted. Giles was proud of the boy. It would have been easy for him to say, "I told you so."

"No?" Buffy looked at him with a hard, angry expression. "I invited him into my home. And even after I knew who he was—what he was—I didn't do anything about it because I had *feelings for him*. Because I cared about him."

"If you care about somebody," Willow offered, with a quick glance at Xander, "you care about them. You can't change that by—"

"Killing them?" Buffy demanded. "Maybe not. But it's a start."

There was a silence. Xander said, "We'll keep an eye on your mom."

Giles knew he had to speak up. He wasn't sure she could beat Angel.

"Buffy—"

She looked up at him. "You can't stop me. The Three found me near the Bronze and so did he. He lives nearby."

Giles persisted. "This is no ordinary vampire." He glanced around and lowered his voice to a whisper. "If there is such a thing. He knows you. He's faced the Three. I think this is going to take more than a simple stake."

"So do I," she bit off.

Giles said no more. He knew her mind was made up. He was very sorry and very worried. But then, he spent most nights worrying about Buffy. What decent human being would not?

In the darkened library, Buffy loaded the crossbow with three bolts. She tested the resistance of the bow. It was a good weapon.

It would do the job.

* * *

In his apartment, Angel was circled by Darla like a predator as he sat slumped in a chair. In a soft, insinuating voice, she purred, "She's out hunting you right now. She wants to kill you."

Angel wanted to kill Darla, do anything to silence her. He only said, "Leave me alone."

"What did you think?" she pressed, leaning into him. "Did you think she would *understand?* That she would look at your face—your true face—and give you a kiss?"

She came close enough to kiss him herself. They gazed at one another, man at woman, monster at monster.

Two of a kind.

Buffy aimed at a poster of a cute guy smoking a cigarette. The caption read, "Smoking sucks." She let the bolt fly, straight into the cancer-ridden guy's heart.

Still Darla pushed Angel. She didn't see, or didn't care, that his anger was building. "For a hundred years you've not had a moment's peace, because you will not accept who you are. That's all you have to do. Accept it. Don't let her hunt you down. Don't whimper and mewl like a mangy human. Kill. Feed. *Live.*"

Her words were the final trigger. He rose and slammed her against the wall, holding her wrists. He spat out, "All right!"

She instantly grew serious, perhaps seeing the

animal behind his eyes as it prepared to spring. Breathing hard, she asked, "What do you want?"

"I want it finished," he said savagely.

"That's good." She slid her glance to his hands around her wrists. "You're hurting me." She smiled. "That's good, too."

Buffy prowled through town. She walked past a vacant lot bordered with a barbed wire fence. Then she neared the Bronze. It was deserted. A small chalkboard sign next to the entrance read, Closed for fumigation. Opening bash this Saturday.

She heard the sound of glass breaking somewhere above her. She looked up, then moved along the side of the Bronze. A metal utility ladder was attached to the wall.

She started to climb.

His thoughts on Buffy, Giles sat beside Joyce Summers's hospital bed, whose thoughts were also about her daughter. "She talks about you all the time," she told him. "It's important to have teachers who make an impression."

He smiled gently and said, "She makes quite an impression herself."

"I know she's having trouble with history. Is it too difficult for her or is she not applying herself?"

And here was the predicament of both Slayer and Watcher—continuing to live their public lives because these things must matter, or there was no point in trying so hard to be normal people. He said to her, as tactfully as possible, "She lives very much in the now, and history, of course, is very much about the then. But there's no reason—"

"She's studying with Willow. She's studying with Darla," Buffy's mother continued. "I mean, she *is* trying."

Giles went on instant alert. "Darla?" he said carefully. "I don't believe I know—"

"Her friend. The one who came over tonight," she filled in, not picking up on his anxiety.

"Darla came to your house tonight? She was the friend that you mentioned earlier?" *Not Angel?*

"Poor thing." Buffy's mother flashed him an embarrassed smile. "I probably frightened her half to death when I fainted. Someone should really check and make sure she's all right."

"Yes. Someone should. Right away." He headed for the door. "I'll do it."

As he left the room, he heard her murmur, "That school is *amazing.*"

Moving quickly, he sped down the hospital corridor. Willow and Xander, who had been waiting outside Ms. Summers's room, joined him.

He said urgently, "We have a problem."

Buffy let herself into the Bronze through a broken window. Crossbow in hand, she searched the balcony, then took the stairs one at a time, sweeping the area with her gaze.

As she reached the main floor of the Bronze, she thought she saw the silhouette of a man some distance away. But when she spun around and took aim, there was no one there.

No *thing* there.

She continued her hunt, moving in the dark stillness. Stripped of lights, people, and noise, the Bronze was an eerie, otherworldly place.

A battleground.

She heard a crash of broken glass and aimed into the darkness again.

"I know you're there," she called out, sweeping the area with the bow. "And I know what you are."

"Do you?" As she zeroed in, Angel spoke again, but this time his voice came from a different location. "I'm just an animal, right?"

"You're not an animal," Buffy said. "Animals I like."

She quickly shifted her weapon. Then her eyes widened as he stepped forward, very close. He wore his vampire face.

He growled. "Let's get it done."

He leaped, moving extremely fast. It took her a moment to adjust to his speed, and by then he had hit the nearby pool table. She brought the crossbow up, sighted, and fired, but the bolt flew across the club and lodged in the far wall as Angel vaulted straight up into the balcony.

Buffy reloaded the bow, crept around the pool table, and aimed up into the darkness. She searched for him, turning slowly. Her heart was thundering. Every sense was on full alert; every Slayer reflex was hair-trigger—

He dropped down behind her, slamming his feet against her neck and sending her flying onto the pool table. Bracing herself against it, she rammed her boot into him with a roundhouse kick, knocking him backward.

While he was out of commission, Buffy scrambled off the pool table and slid onto the floor, reaching for her crossbow. She rolled onto her back and raised up slightly, pointed the deadly weapon at Angel, and kept him in her sights.

He rose, and faced her, presenting her with the perfect shot.

He growled.

Her finger tightened on the trigger.

Then Angel's appearance morphed from his vampire features into the handsome young man who had so attracted her when they had first met. Who had battled beside her against the Three.

"Come on," he said in a hard voice. "Don't go soft on me now."

Buffy let the bolt fly. It missed him by a mile and sank into the post beside him.

"A little wide," he observed.

They looked at each other. "Why?" she asked quietly, getting to her feet, her voice shaking with anger. "Why didn't you just attack me when you had the chance? Was it a joke? To make me feel for you and then . . ." She stopped herself for a split-second. "I've killed a lot of vampires. I've never *hated* one before."

"Feels good, doesn't it?" he asked, also quietly, also emotionally. "Feels simple."

"I invited you into my home," she went on, needing to express her hurt, feeling again her shock and despair. "And then you attacked my family."

"Why not?" he asked almost offhandedly, but his expression was filled with pain. "I killed mine."

He started closing in on her.

"I killed their friends. And their friends' children. For a hundred years I offered an ugly death to everyone I met. And I did it with a song in my heart."

She detected the merest hint of self-loathing; she raised her chin slightly and asked, "What changed?"

"Fed on a girl," he told her. "About your age. Beautiful." He looked off into the distance for a moment. "Dumb as a post. But a favorite among her clan."

"Her clan?" Buffy repeated, unsure of his word choice.

"Romani," he explained. "Gypsies. The elders conjured the perfect punishment for me." He waited a beat. "They restored my soul."

"What," she asked, regaining a bit of her fire, "they were all out of boils and blinding torment?"

"When you become a vampire, the demon takes your body but it doesn't get your soul. That's gone. No conscience, no remorse. It's an easy way to live."

She remembered how he had asked her if it felt good to hate him. Simple.

He stood in the weak light, surrounded by darkness, facing an armed Slayer who was bent on revenge. And yet he made no move to attack, nor to escape. Instead, he said, "You have no idea what it's like to have done the things I've done and to care. I haven't fed on a living human being since that day."

"So you started with my mom?" she flung at him.

"I didn't bite her," he said very seriously.

She was taken aback. "Then why didn't you say something?"

"I wanted to." For a moment Buffy tried to pretend that he was answering her question. But he was confessing that he had wanted to bite her mother. As if to underscore that thought, he said, "I can walk like a man but I'm not one." He paused. "I wanted to kill you tonight."

She knew that. She had wanted to kill him, too. She looked down, laid down her weapon, and walked to him, tilting her head slightly, offering her neck.

"Go ahead," she said. With all her heart, she prayed he would not attack her. With all her soul, she believed he wouldn't, and yet, every ounce of her being protested the way she left herself defenseless. She was the Slayer, and he was a vampire.

He remained silent, gazing at her with his haunted eyes. Something lifted for a brief instant as the two of them stared long and hard at each other.

She nodded slightly. "Not as easy as it looks," she said.

He almost smiled.

"Sure it is," came a voice from the shadows.

Xander, Willow, and Giles raced through the night, searching for Buffy.

Willow said, "We're near the Bronze. What now?"

Giles answered, "Keep looking for her."

"I have a question," Xander ventured, worried and frustrated. "What if we find her and she's fighting Angel or some of his friends? What the heck are *we* going to do about it?"

No one answered.

No one had an answer.

Darla strolled toward Angel and Buffy with her hands clasped behind her back, as if she hadn't a care in the world. She drawled, "Do you know what the saddest thing in the world is?"

Buffy shrugged. "Bad hair on top of that outfit?"

"To love someone who used to love you." She glared at Buffy.

Buffy glanced in surprise at Angel. "You guys were . . . involved?"

"For *several* generations." Darla clearly enjoyed telling Buffy all this.

Buffy tried to regroup. She remembered Darla now. She was the one who had lured Xander's friend Jesse to the cemetary on Buffy's first night in Sunnydale. *She* led Jesse to his death. "Well, when you've been around since Columbus, you're bound to pile up a few exes. You *are* older than him, right?" She leaned forward, sneering at Darla. "Just between us girls, you're looking a little worn around the eyes."

Darla bared her fangs in an evil smile. "I made him," she said triumphantly, as if she knew this would be even harder for Buffy to hear. "And there was a time when we shared everything." She focused her full attention on Angel. "Wasn't there, Angelus?"

Angel said nothing. Darla's smile faded. "You had a chance to come home. To rule with me in the Master's court for a thousand years. But you threw that away because of her." She said in disbelief, "You love someone who hates us."

Buffy tried to hide her surprise. *Angel loves me? Had he told Darla? How else would she know?*

She glanced at Angel, who looked worriedly back at her. *Because he's afraid for me? Or afraid for me to know he cares about me?*

"You're sick," Darla told Angel. "And you'll always be sick, and you'll always remember what it was like to watch her die." She spoke in a singsong tone very like the Master's.

She turned to Buffy, saying, "You don't think I came alone, do you?"

Buffy replied, "I know I didn't." With a flash of movement, she stomped on the crossbow, sending it flying up into her hands.

Darla chuckled. "Scary," she admitted. From behind her back, she brought forward two enormous revolvers——.357s, Buffy guessed; they hadn't studied firearms much—and pointed them directly at her.

"Scar*ier,*" she said, and began firing with both hands.

Buffy dove under the pool table. Angel took a bullet to the shoulder and slammed into the wall with the crossbow bolt stuck into it. With a grunt of pain, he slid to the floor.

"Angel!" Buffy cried.

"Oh, don't worry," Darla said easily. "Bullets can't kill vampires. They can hurt them like hell, but—"

She fired at Buffy again.

In the warehouse alley, Xander and the others froze.

"Did you just hear—"

Gunshots. They all heard them.

They all ran toward the Bronze.

Buffy crouched behind the pool table, listening to Darla rant as she closed in. "So many body parts, so few bullets. Let's begin with the kneecaps. No fun dancing without them . . ."

Bullets hailed in Buffy's direction. Buffy summoned her courage, popped up, and got off a crossbow shot. It slammed into Darla's chest, and Darla doubled forward. For a moment, Buffy thought she was home free. She spared a glance in Angel's direction. He was pulling himself up by holding on to the crossbow bolt in the wall.

Then Darla straightened back up. She said, "Close. But no heart."

She pulled the bolt out of her chest and dropped it onto the floor.

Willow, Giles, and Xander entered the Bronze through the broken window on the second floor and made their way to the balcony. They all looked in horror at the destruction below.

Xander whispered, "We need to distract her." He saw at the same time that Buffy did that Buffy was out of bolts. "Fast!"

Willow shouted frantically, "Buffy, it wasn't Angel who attacked your mom. It was Darla!"

Darla whirled in their direction, raining bullets on them. They ducked.

On the main floor of the Bronze, Angel, breathing hard through the pain, pulled the crossbow bolt out of the wall.

Darla jumped and landed with both feet on the pool table. Buffy rose and yanked the table toward her, knocking Darla off balance. Darla slammed onto her back as Buffy now pushed the table with all her might. Darla's guns blazed as the table flew backward; she tracked Buffy's course as Buffy ran to the Bronze's coffee counter and threw herself over it. The glass case shattered above her.

A distraction.

Giles spied a light board nearby. He scrambled

over and started pounding and punching the buttons. Spot lights flashed on, and then a pulsating strobe.

For a moment, the vampire named Darla was disoriented, and Giles rejoiced. But then she advanced on Buffy again, her movements nightmarishly jerky in the strobe's relentless flash. She fired at Buffy, who was huddled behind the bar. Upsidedown glassware exploded like crystalline land mines as Buffy dodged the bullets.

"Come on, Buffy," Darla urged. "Take it like a man."

Darla fired again, grinning, delighted, as if victory was almost hers. And then, in the wild strobe light, Giles saw Angel behind her, a crossbow bolt in his hand. He rose without warning and plunged the arrow into Darla's back.

Giles shut off the strobe. All that remained was moonlight and silence.

Darla staggered. The guns clattered to the floor. She turned.

"Angel?" she murmured in disbelief.

She grabbed onto him for a moment, but only a moment. Angel watched as she collapsed, then exploded into a scream and dust.

His sire. His lover. She had made him, but someone had made her into a demon first. And no one had given her back her soul. And, in the old days, how they had raged together. It was she who had given him the Gypsy girl, never dreaming it would mean the end of them, or that it would bring them to this night when he would destroy her forever.

Buffy, the beautiful and courageous human who loved him, rose from behind the counter and looked at Angel with huge eyes. He didn't know what to say to her. He wasn't sure he could speak. With the death of Darla, he had crossed many lines. He had gone too far. And he could never go back.

Slowly, he turned and walked away.

The Master howled with rage and despair. He wielded his killing spear in blind fury, smashing whatever lay in his path, sweeping an enormous candelabra to the floor of his prison. He raged in a frenzy, until finally, overcome with grief, he fell to the ground.

"Darla," he wept.

The Anointed One approached him, perfectly calm. He said, "Forget her."

One last ounce of outrage flashed through the Master as he looked at his secret weapon and said, "How dare you. She was my favorite. For four hundred years—"

"She was weak," his young warrior stated flatly. "We don't need her. *I'll* bring you the Slayer."

The Master was spent, dejected. "But to lose her to Angel. He was to sit on my right come the day. And now . . ." He trailed off.

"They're all against you," Collin said. "But soon

you shall rise, and when you do . . ." He gently rubbed the Master's shoulder and offered him his hand. "We'll kill them all."

The Master was comforted. Managing a brave smile, he took the Anointed One's outstretched hand and squeezed it.

EPILOGUE

Buffy felt odd returning to the Bronze. Open for business again, it was packed with people, music, and laughter. So different from the last time she had been here.

And the last time she had seen Angel.

She wore the cross he had given her the first night they had met. It was a treasured possession now, proof that he wasn't like all the other vampires in her strange, scary world.

Xander said with mock enthusiasm, "Ah, the postfumigation party."

Buffy asked, "What's the difference between this and the prefumigation party?"

Xander replied, "Much heartier cockroaches."

Buffy couldn't help but look around for Angel. Willow must have noticed, for she said kindly, "No word from Angel?"

Buffy tried for a light tone. "Naw. It's weird, though. In a way I feel like he's still watching me."

Willow kept smiling. She said, "Well, in a way, he sort of is. In the way that he's right over there."

Buffy and Xander turned at the exact same time. Buffy composed herself and walked toward the vampire she loved.

Willow saw the dashed look on Xander's face. As they reached a table, he deliberately chose the chair that faced away from Buffy and Angel.

He said, "I don't need to watch because I'm not threatened. I'm just going to look *this* way."

Angel stood alone, as always. Though she was set apart as the Slayer, Buffy knew she had so much more than he did: her friends, her Watcher, her mother . . . and a chance, now and then, to blow off some steam. Angel had none of this. And she suspected that now that he had killed Darla, the vampire who had changed him, he would be hunted as fiercely as she was.

Thinking all these things, and of how much she loved him, Buffy came to him.

For a moment, neither spoke. Then Angel said, "I just wanted to see if you were okay. And your mother."

"We're both good. You?"

He laughed shortly. "If I can go a little while without being shot or stabbed, I'll be all right." Then he hesitated, as if that wasn't true. "Look," he said, "this can't—"

"Ever be anything," she finished for him. "I know." And she did know. She tried to conceal her pain with a joke. "For one thing, you're like two hundred and twenty-four years older than I am."

His smile was faint, as if he appreciated her attempt to make this easy on both of them. "I just have to . . . I have to walk away from this."

Buffy said, almost in a whisper, "I know. Me, too."

They stood staring at each other. Hesitantly, she added, "One of us has to go here."

"I know."

Still neither left. Then Angel bent his head to kiss her. She kissed him back, willing warmth into his cold, soft lips, thrilling at the tenderness of his kiss. She put her arms around his neck and allowed herself this moment, even if she never saw him again.

Xander demanded, "What's going on?" He was obviously dying of curiosity . . . and jealousy, Willow had to admit to herself, but she bet herself an extra hour of surfing on the Net tonight that he would not succumb and turn around.

"Nothing," she assured him, acting as lookout.

"Well, as long as they're not kissing." He laughed uncomfortably.

Willow said nothing, only smiled as her best friend, the Vampire Slayer, lost herself in Angel's arms.

* * *

The kiss ended. Buffy looked up at Angel and asked gently, "Are you okay?"

He seemed to struggle for words. "It's just . . ."

Her eyes welled. "Painful. I know." Then she summoned the courage to say what must be said, "See you around?"

She turned and walked away.

And pain played over the face of Angel, born into the night as Angelus, as he watched the Slayer go. But her mark was on him: the cross she wore around her neck—the cross he himself had given her—had burned deep and hot into his chest.

As his love for her burned deep and hot into his soul.

THE SECOND CHRONICLE:

REPTILE BOY

PROLOGUE

It was not a quiet night for the Slayer. A high-pitched wailing rose incessantly around her, reminding her of some demon, vampire, or other monster in the chocolate box that was the Hellmouth, begging for its life.

And echoing this thought, Xander asked, concerned, "Is she dying?"

He and Buffy lounged on Buffy's bed on either side of Willow, who sat on the floor clutching a cow doll as her friends braided her hair and stared in wonderment at the TV.

And on said TV, thanks to the glory of cable and its many offspring, the fringe channels of the night—what music they make!—the three stared without much comprehension at an Indian woman as she warbled in a very personally meaningful way into her telephone.

Buffy said in awe, "I think she's singing."

Xander ran with that. "To a telephone, in Hindi. Now that's entertainment." He stared. "Why is she singing?"

Willow, wide-eyed, solved the puzzle. "She's sad because her lover gave her twelve gold coins but then the wizard cut open the bag of salt and now the dancing minions have no place to put their big Maypole . . ." she gestured, as if searching for the right word, "fish thing."

"Uh-huh," Xander said, still staring. "Why is she *singing?*"

Buffy was likewise stumped. "Her lover? I thought that was her chiropractor."

Willow never took her eyes off the screen. "Because of that thing he did with her feet? No. That was personal."

The piercing singing was apparently in no danger of approaching a grand finale. Xander said, "And we thought 'cause we didn't have any money or anyplace to go, this'd be a lackluster evening."

Willow brightened. "I know! We could go to the Bronze, sneak in our own tea bags, and ask for hot water."

Xander smiled faintly. "Hop off the outlaw train, Will, before you land us all in jail."

Buffy cut in, "I, for one, am giddy and up. There's a kind of hush all over Sunnydale, no demons or vampires to slay, I'm here with my friends," she leaned toward the TV, "so how does the water buffalo fit in again?"

* * *

Across town, there was no singing in a sprawling, two-story California stucco mansion. The stillness of the night was shattered as a pretty girl crashed through the door on the second story, flung herself over the balcony, tumbled to a vast expanse of manicured lawn, and ran for her life.

A hooded figure darted from the ruined door onto the balcony, looked down, and ran back into the house. Within seconds, several dark figures in hooded robes emerged from other windows and doors like malevolent wraiths and chased the fleeing girl.

Panting with fear and exertion, the girl bolted into the woods. She ran fast, but her pursuers were faster. They were closing the gap between them as she darted under tree branches and flew over roots. Under a large tree, she fell and rolled, then got to her feet and heaved herself up onto a stone wall with all her might.

As she dropped down to the other side, three hooded figures clambered over the wall right behind her.

She flew through the graveyard now, the moonlight highlighting the nightmarish setting and the names on the stones. *Home free,* she prayed, as she passed a strange, pyramid-shaped crypt. *I am going to live.*

Then suddenly, another robed figure stepped out from behind a monument and grabbed her. She screamed and struggled against him.

"Callie," the figure chided her. "Callie, where are you going?"

It was Richard, the good-looking blond boy who had enticed her to the frat house with the promise of a good time. "The party's just getting started," he continued easily.

Then, as the other figures caught up to them, he threw her into their arms. They began to drag her away. Tears rolled down her cheeks as she struggled for her life.

Richard looked around to make sure they had not been seen. Then he put on his hood and slowly followed the others as they returned their prey to her prison.

CHAPTER 1

The night of Hindi telephone wailing was over.

The day of Sunnydale High wailing had just begun.

"Ha-ha ha-ha, oh, mmm. See?" Cordelia demonstrated for one of her Cordettes. Cordelia was holding a magazine folded open to a particular section. She explained to her faithful follower, "Doctor Debbi says when a man is speaking, you make serious eye contact and you really, really listen. And you laugh at everything he says." Again, she demonstrated: "Ha-ha ha-ha ha-ha."

Eager for details, Willow asked Buffy as the two headed downstairs, "You dreamed about Angel again?"

"Third night in a row," Buffy said, somewhere between embarrassed and eager to share.

"What did he do in the dream?" Willow prodded.

Buffy grinned dreamily—some might say goofily. "Stuff."

"Ooh, stuff," Willow said excitedly. "Was it one of those vivid dreams where you could feel his lips and smell his hair?"

Buffy nodded. "It had surround-sound." She sighed. "I'm just thinking about him so much lately."

When she returned from summer vacation in L.A. with her father, she had told Angel she had moved on "to the living." It had been a lie, of course. She was afraid of her future. If she couldn't protect herself, how could she ever protect her friends? She had been cruel to him, pushing him—and Willow, Xander, and even Giles—away because she had finally managed to kill the Master, but in doing so had died at his hands herself. "Technically," as Giles would put it. The Master had bitten her, and then she had drowned. But she *had* died.

Xander had revived her, and she'd gone on to battle the Master again, to the death. But it wasn't an experience one could easily get over.

And she had been so afraid to come back to Sunnydale—to come back to the life of danger for her friends—that she had even baited Angel to take her on, vampire against Slayer. He would have none of it. And when she finally broke, it was to Angel she turned. He had wrapped his arms around her and let her sob out all her anger and terror.

More recently, he had even admitted his jealousy of Xander, who could walk in the daylight with her.

So why didn't they have a thing going? He kept

showing up, they'd have some kind of fight or intense encounter, and then he was gone again.

"You two are so right for each other," Willow gushed, "except for the, uh—"

"Vampire thing." Buffy said it. Someone had to.

"That doesn't make him a bad person," Willow said loyally. Apparently she was not about to give up on this grand romance. "Necessarily." But she was willing to give a little ground on whether or not it was a good idea.

"I'm brainsick!" Buffy cried. "I can't have a relationship with him."

"Not during the day, but you could ask him for coffee some night." Buffy looked at her. Willow persisted. "It's the non-relationship drink of choice. It's not a date, it's a caffeinated beverage. Okay, sure, it's hot and bitter, like a relationship that way, but—"

Xander slid into step with them.

"What's like a relationship?" he asked cheerily.

"Nothing *I* have." Buffy gave Willow another look, this one more speculative. "Coffee?"

As they neared that wacky reality field where Cordelia and her gal pals reigned supreme, Buffy and Willow peeled off. Xander, however, slowed to catch something he could riff off. He was not disappointed, as Cordelia said to her little clone wannabe, "There's really no comparison between college men and high school boys." She gave Xander a disdainful once-over. "I mean, look at *that.*"

All right. The gauntlet had been thrown. Xander

said pleasantly, "So, Cor, you dating college guys now?"

She preened like a little peacock hen, styling her sculpted bangs as she bragged, "Well, not that it's any of your business, but I happen to be dating a Delta Zeta Kappa."

"Oh, an extraterrestrial," he quipped. "So that's how you get a date after you've exhausted all the human guys."

At the water fountain, Buffy and Willow listened.

"You'll go to college someday, Xander," Cordelia said sincerely. Then she shot home the zinger: "I just know your pizza delivery career will take you so many exciting places."

Xander didn't know what to say. He had no comeback. A bit startled, he joined up with his nicer friends as they loitered by the watering hole. He was about to say something funny to them to show that Cordelia hadn't affected him when the bell rang.

Buffy made a face. "Ooooh, I told Giles I'd meet him in the library ten minutes ago." She shrugged. "Oh, he won't be upset. There hasn't been much paranormal activity lately."

Wrong. Giles circled her like some old English judge wearing one of those white bad-perm wigs in a movie about burning people at the stake and gave her the old one-two.

"Just because the paranormal is more normal and less . . . para of late, is no excuse for tardiness or letting your guard down."

She was maybe the taddiest bit defensive. "I haven't let my guard down."

"Oh, really?" he drawled. He circled back the other way. "You yawned your way through weapons training last week. You skipped the hand-to-hand entirely." Now he stood behind her. "Are you going to be prepared if a demon springs up behind you and does *this?*"

Without warning, he swung at her from behind. She grabbed his wrist, pivoted, and whipped his hand behind his back. One more upward yank, and she could break it without so much as breathing hard.

Giles grunted in pain. "Yes, well, I'm not a demon." He grunted again. "Which is why you should let go now."

Without blinking, Buffy complied. "Thank you," he muttered. He straightened, massaging his wrist. He no longer looked annoyed with her, but he did look concerned.

Buffy sat on the table as he wound up for the pitch.

"When you live atop a mystical convergence, it's only a matter of time before a fresh hell breaks lose," he told her. "Now is the time to train more strictly. You should hunt and patrol more keenly. You should hone your skills day and night."

Buffy was so tired of all this. She cut in, "And the little slice of my life that still belongs to me—from, I don't know, seven to seven-oh-five in the morning, can I do what I want to then?"

Giles looked frustrated, yet there was a bit of compassion—the merest bit—as he said, "Buffy, you think I don't know what it's like to be sixteen?"

"No," she retorted, "I think you don't know what it's like to be sixteen and a girl and the Slayer."

"Fair enough," he had to admit. He took off his glasses and rubbed his eyes. "No, I don't."

Her voice rose. "Or what it's like to have to stake vampires when you're having fuzzy feelings toward one?"

"Ahhh," he said awkwardly.

"Digging on the undead doesn't exactly do wonders for your social life."

He pounced like the Bengal tiger that had gone after the Hindi Telephone Woman's water buffalo. "That's exactly where being different comes in handy."

"Right," she said, kinda sorta wishing he'd circle her again so she could almost break his arm again. "Who needs a social life when they've got their very own Hellmouth?"

"Yes!" Clearly he had missed her sarcastic tone. "You have a duty, a purpose! You have a commitment in life. How many people your age do you think can say that?"

How many want to? she almost shot back, but that would reactivate his lecture mode. Instead, she lifted her chin and said, "We talkin' foreign or domestic? How about *none.*"

Giles sighed. Sometimes he didn't know why he tried. Flaring—just a trifle, although God knew he had his own pressures to deal with—he snapped,

"Well, here's a hard fact of life. We all have to do things we don't like. And you have hand to hand this afternoon and patrol tonight. So I suggest you come straight here at the end of period six and get your homework done. And don't dawdle with your friends."

Buffy thrust out her lower lip, letting her chin quiver like a sad little girl. He hardened his heart. He said these things for her own good. "And don't think sitting there pouting is going to get to me. Because it won't."

The chin quivered. The brows lifted. She was only sixteen. She did have a point.

"It's not getting to me," he insisted.

Free at last.

Willow and Xander moseyed with the rest of the herd out of Sunnydale High. Xander said, "Boy, was that a long day."

Willow replied archly, "And you skipped three classes."

"Yeah, and of course *they* flew by." He looked up and cried, "Buffy!"

Before them, Buffy sat on the stair railing and dangled her shoes. She was wearing her sunglasses and she looked cool. She smiled as they approached.

Willow said gently, "Aren't you supposed to be doing your homework in the library?"

Buffy grinned at her. "I'm dawdling. With my friends." Playfully she caught Xander's arm between her own and cosied up to him.

"Works for me," Xander said happily.

Just then, Cordelia, in a mad dash to make some kind of grand exit or grand entrance, bashed into Willow and didn't even register it. As the Scooby Gang mumbled about her bad manners, she tripped down the stairs.

A very wicked-lovely black BMW, fully loaded with a moon roof and all the other good stuff, pulled up to the curb. From where she dawdled, Buffy could see Cordelia's reflection perfectly mirrored in the sleek black exterior as the self-proclaimed Slayer of Dating took off her sunglasses like an aspiring spokesmodel and flashed her very large smile at the tinted window.

Oh, God. He had driven his Beemer to see her and *everything.* The tinted window rolled down and there he was, handsome, wealthy Richard Anderson, and he spoke the magic word: her name.

"Cordelia."

She smiled hugely at him and never blinked, just as Doctor Debbi instructed. "Hi, Richard. Nice car."

Some guy was sitting next to him, not as cute, not as fashionable. Cordelia didn't pay any attention to him as Richard said, "So, we're having a little get together tomorrow night at the house."

The house. Their fraternity house. She followed his lips, his eyes, his dimples. He glanced at his friend, then to wherever his friend was looking. But that was okay. As long as she didn't look elsewhere she was doing what she was supposed to.

Richard was saying, "And it's going to be a really special evening."

Now, Cordelia told herself, and let forth with a lovely trill of laughter: "Ha-ha ha-ha."

Richard blinked and said, "Excuse me?"

Mmm. She had laughed wrong. Recovering, she renewed her efforts to never take her eyes off his face and said, "Oh, I'd love, *love* to!"

Richard looked past her again. "Who's your friend?"

Cordelia turned. Buffy was smiling and laughing at some idiotic thing that loser Xander was saying. She did a mental double-take. *What?* Did he actually mean Buffy the Chosen Psycho-loony?

"Her? Oh, she's not my friend," Cordelia announced.

Richard's friend spoke for the first time. "She's amazing."

"She's more like a sister, really," Cordelia amended without missing a beat. "We're that close."

Richard smiled at her—at Cordelia, the girl he was supposed to smile at—and said, "Why don't you introduce us?"

Fuming on the inside, gazing and smiling for all she was worth, or rather, all *Richard* was worth, on the outside, Cordelia gritted, "Okay."

Xander said, "Okay. So tonight, channel fifty-nine. Indian TV—sex, lies, incomprehensible story lines. I'll bring the betel nuts."

Buffy was psyched. Another quiet evening with

her two best friends and something weird but not fatal. Her happy little notion of heaven.

Just then Cordelia walked up, grabbed Buffy, and started to haul her away. "Come on," she hissed. "Richard and his fraternity brother want to meet you."

Buffy stood her ground. "Well, I don't really want to meet any fraternity boys."

Cordelia gave her a venomous look. "And if there was a God, don't you think He'd keep it that way?"

Cordelia renewed her hauling.

"Hey," Xander called after them, "I believe we were dawdling here."

And here was Cordy's love slave out of his rich kid's car. He flashed a full set of bonded porcelain at Buffy and said, "Hi, sweetheart. I'm Richard. And you are?"

"So not interested," she said with feeling. She turned to leave. She only had a few minutes of freedom left, and she most definitely did not want to waste it on this Ken doll.

Cordelia grabbed her wrist. "She's such a little comedienne!" she chirped, digging her acrylics into Buffy's upper arm.

"What, she likes to play hard to get?" Richard asked.

"No, Richard." This was the other guy who had been in the Beemer. "I think you're playing easy to resist." With that as her getaway line, Buffy walked away.

The other guy stepped shyly in front of her and said, "Feel free to ignore him. I do all the time."

Buffy hesitated. This guy seemed a little more normal.

"I'm Tom Warner," he said. "I'm a senior at Crestwood College and I feel just like a complete dolt meeting you this way." He crossed his arms. "So here I stand in all my doltishness."

Xander, eavesdropping, said to Willow, who was also eavesdropping, "Right. Like she's gonna fall for that."

Okay, I won't stake him, Buffy thought. Here was a guy who talked the nice talk. Who was actually being real. Who truly seemed interested in her.

"I'm Buffy Summers," she told him.

"Nice to meet you. Are you a senior?"

She wasn't fooled . . . maybe, but it was nice of him to pay her the compliment anyway. "Junior."

"Me, too," he said brightly, "except that I'm a senior, and I'm in college." He grinned. "So we have that in common." Then he added, "And I major in history."

"Mmm. History stumps me," Buffy admitted. "I have a hard enough time remembering what happened last week."

"Nothing happened last week. Don't worry. I was there," he assured her.

Buffy smiled, making a mental list of Tom's attributes: Witty. Friendly. Liking her. Not so bad, for a frat boy.

* * *

Xander said to Willow: "She's going to walk away. Now."

Tom must have sensed that Buffy was defrosting around the edges, because he said, "So my friend asked your friend to this party we're having tomorrow night."

As if that were a huge, entertaining notion, Cordelia's most-fake laughter rang out across the land: "Ha-ha ha-ha ha-ha."

He lowered his voice. "You know, actually he's not really my friend. I only joined the fraternity because my father and grampa were in it before me. It meant a lot to them."

Xander was still sending his masterful ESP waves to Buffy: "Okay, boots, start a-walkin'."

"I know, I talk too much. Anyway," Tom went on, "they're really dull parties full of really dull people, so would you like to come and save me from a really dull fate?"

Temptworthy, she decided, but she said sincerely, "Oh, I wish I could, but I'm sort of involved."

"Oh." He was let down. "Sure. Of course you are. Well, thanks for letting me ramble."

Buffy was sorry. She said warmly, "You know, people underestimate the value of a good ramble."

He smiled, grateful for her attempt to take the sting out the rejection.

"Buffy!" Giles called, clearly irritated.

Buffy turned. He was standing near the front door of the school, tapping his watch.

"Oh, I gotta go," she told Tom. "It was nice to meet you." She meant it.

His smile was genuine, friendly, unsmarmy. "Same here."

Willow nodded to Buffy as Buffy scurried away. The fraternity guy she'd been talking to was still looking at her, obviously intrigued. Willow sighed inwardly. Must be nice. Scary, though. Those older guys.

Beside her, Xander shook his head. He was clearly disgusted. "I hate these guys. Whatever they want just falls into their laps. Don't you hate these guys?"

Willow nodded absently. "Yeah, with their charmed lives and their movie star good looks and more money than you can count . . ." Then she realized she was probably punching Xander in the macho plexus, so she assured him, "I'm hating."

What was wrong with the girl? All his efforts to prepare her for her duty as a Slayer seemed to go for naught. How did the Americans so charmingly put it? She continually blew him off.

Giles couldn't keep his irritation out of his voice as he faced her, he in arm guards, she in a thinnish shirt and sweat pants. He said, "I'm going to attack you. Word of caution: for your own good, I won't be pulling any punches."

She said defiantly, "Please don't."

He rushed her with a short sword. She kicked it

out of his hand. Immediately he countered with a wooden rod, which she broke in half with her foot without so much as blinking.

He lunged. She sidestepped. He slid past her on the tabletop.

Drat it all. He was only reinforcing her belief that she didn't need to practice. "Good," he bit off. "So you're on patrol and I'll see you in the morning."

Unless something happened to her.

Sometimes he wanted to shake her. Shake some sense into that keen mind, so muddled by the vast cultural wasteland in which she lived.

Day was done, and Buffy was on patrol.

Cloaked by the black night, she moved through the shadows in the graveyard, alert, ready, checking the stakes in her belt. She had the sense that someone was watching her. That was fine with her. She'd like something to wallop the tar out of, since she couldn't wallop Giles.

She moved on, as cautious as always, despite what Giles had to say about sloppy Slayage habits. He had his nerve, lecturing her. Who was the Slayer, anyway? Who put her life on the line every night while he read his musty old books?

The moonlight glinted off something on the ground. She knelt to examine it. It was a piece of a very small and delicate ID bracelet. She studied it, turning it in the dim light. There were three initials, *E, N,* and *T* engraved in a delicate scroll.

"There's blood on it," said a voice.

She started, then turned and relaxed. Sort of. Angel towered over her and she said in a rush, to hide her joy at seeing him, "Oh, hi. Nice to . . . blood?" She looked questioningly down at the bracelet.

Angel said simply, "I can smell it."

She took that in, but she wasn't sure what to do with it. "It's pretty thin," she observed. "Probably belonged to a girl."

Angel glanced around the woods. "Probably."

She laughed and he looked back at her. "I was just thinking. Wouldn't it be funny to see each other some time when it wasn't a blood thing?" She waited for him to say something. He just stared at her. She added, "Not funny ha ha."

His face hardly changed at all. "What are you saying, you want to have a date?"

"No . . ." Was she saying that? And what would be wrong with a date, anyway? After all they'd been through together—

After the way he'd kissed her; after the dreams she'd had about him—

"You don't want to have a date," he stated.

Hey, wait, don't shut that door, she thought anxiously. "Who said date? I never said date."

"Right, you just want to have coffee or something." What, was he a mind reader? How did he know about—

"Coffee?" she echoed.

"I knew this would happen." He sounded kind of tired. Or resigned.

"What? What do you think is happening?" Her voice was high and shrill. She had to lower it. She had to be cooler.

"You're sixteen years old. I'm two hundred and forty-one."

Ouch, ouch, ouch. "I've done the math," she said, trying not to sound like two-hundred and forty-one minus sixteen was two hundred and twenty-five.

"You don't know what you're doing, you don't know what you want," he went on, crushing everything crushable about her ego. He sounded so above it all. He sounded like *he* sure as heck wasn't having dreams about *her*. Or maybe like he knew what he didn't want.

"Oh, no?" she asked. "I think I do. I want out of this conversation." She turned to walk away. He grabbed her and looked at her very hard.

"Listen, if we date, you and I both know one thing's going to lead to another."

It was a moment between them like other moments they had had. Slayer, vampire; girl, guy. It was mixed up. She was mixed up. But she did know one thing: Angel was in her life whether she wanted it or not, and whether he realized it or not.

"One thing already has led to another," she shot back. "Don't you think it's a little late to be reading me the warning label?"

"I'm just trying to protect you." He was very serious. Very close. She wanted him to kiss her. She wanted all the things girls wanted from guys they loved. "This could get out of control."

She replied, her face raised toward his, her voice breathy, "Isn't that the way it's supposed to be?"

Without warning, he pulled her roughly against his chest. A thrill shot through her—half excitement, half fear—as she looked up into his angry face. Was he going to kiss her, or attack her? Or for them, was it the same thing?

"This isn't some fairy tale," he said harshly. "When I kiss you, you don't wake up from a deep sleep and live happily ever after."

"No." She knew that. She so knew that. In his arms, so close, so very close, she breathed against his neck and said, "When you kiss me, I want to die."

She held his gaze—hadn't he known that, realized that?—then turned and ran.

Daylight.
School.
Buffy slowly gathered her books off her desk as Cordelia breezed in.

Cordelia said, "Did you lose weight? And your hair . . ." Despite the fact that Buffy was ignoring her, Cordelia gave a little shrug and said, "All right. I respect you too much to be dishonest. The hair's a little . . ."

She laughed. "Well, that's not the point here, is it. The Zeta Kappas have to have a certain balance at their party, and Richard explained it all to me but I was so busy *really listening* that I didn't hear much. Anyway, the deal is they need you to go. And if you don't go"—she touched her chest as her eyes welled—*"I* can't."

Buffy looked at her, then looked down.

"I'm talking about Richard *Anderson,* okay?" Cordelia continued. "As in Anderson Farms, Anderson Aeronautics . . ." She almost burst into tears, "and Anderson *Cosmetics.*"

She caught herself and moved on. "Well, Buffy, you see why I have to go. These men are rich. And I'm not being shallow. Think of all the poor people I could help with all my money."

Buffy said quietly, "I'll go."

"You'll go?" Cordelia's tears instantly dried. "Great! I'll drive. Oh, Buffy, it's just like we're sisters . . . with really different hair!"

Cordelia sailed away. Buffy stared after her, no happier now than before Cordelia had come into the room.

Hooded figures watched among the rocks and candles of the eerie cavern below the Delta Zeta Kappa frat house. It was an ancient place, more a cave than a basement, cut from stone. A large stone stairway led down to it from the frat house main floor. Candles flickered on the walls of a large pit on the far side of the room.

A young man stood naked to the waist, a little eager, a little frightened, as Richard, his hood thrown back, pointed a sword at his chest.

Richard intoned, "I pledge my life, and my death."

The young man repeated, his voice trembling slightly, "I pledge my life and my death."

Richard went on. "To the Delta Zeta Kappas and to Machida, whom we serve." He began to carve a symbol into the young man's chest.

The young man didn't flinch. "To the Delta Zeta Kappas and to Machida, whom we serve."

No one else spoke. Richard's voice rang out as he sliced the young man's chest with the blade, "On my oath, before my assembled brethren."

The young man said, "On my oath, before my assembled brethren."

"I promise to keep our secret from this day until my death," Richard finished.

"I promise to keep our secret from this day until my death," the young man said firmly.

Richard lowered the sword. "In blood I was baptized, in blood I shall reign, in His name!"

The young man was full of fervor. "In blood I was baptized, in blood I shall reign, in His name!"

"You are now one of us," Richard told him.

"In His name," the young man replied, as around him, the others joined in like a chorus, echoing, "In His name."

"Brewski time!" Richard cried.

Suddenly someone opened a cooler and flung mass quantities of beer to the masses. A boom box blared on and the music throbbed. What two seconds before had been a fairly brutal initiation ritual had become a typical frat party, as the frat brothers clapped the young man on the back and congratulated him.

Richard smiled, watching them, then turned his

attention to the girl they had caught trying to escape. She hung in chains from the wall, and she was looking a little the worse for wear.

He said to her, "So what's a nice girl like you doing in a place like this?"

"Let me go," she begged.

He cocked his head in thought. "Let you go? Okay, let me think . . . uh, no."

She burst into tears and he laughed at her. He said, "Gawd, I love high school girls," sipped his beer, and nodded his head to the music. This was the life.

The girl sobbed.

CHAPTER 2

Willow was wide-eyed as she said to Buffy, "You're going to the fraternity party?"

They sat in the school lounge. Xander was officially reading a skateboard magazine but he was actually hanging on every word that passed between Buffy and Willow. They knew it, he knew they knew, it was the way it was.

"What made you change your mind?" Willow asked.

Buffy felt dejected all over again—make that *re*jected—as she said, "Angel."

Willow was even more impressed. "He's going with you?" She said to Xander, "She's got a date with Angel. Isn't that exciting?"

Xander said ironically, "I'm elated."

Buffy knew that no way would they figure out the

rest on their own, so she filled in the blanks. "I'm not going with Angel. I'm going with . . . ye, gods, Cordelia."

"Cordelia?" Willow piped in. "Did I sound a little jealous just then? Because I'm not, really." In the same tone as before, she re-piped, *"Cordelia?"*

Xander cut in. "Cordelia's much better for you than Angel."

As they left the lounge and headed down the hall, Willow asked, "What happened with Angel?"

Buffy almost hated talking about it. She felt kind of stupid, blathering on about her intense dreams the way she had, then remembering his I-need-to-protect-you-from-my-savage-need monologue. She could stake vampires from now to doomsday. She could manage to keep her life as a career slaying machine a secret, even from her mom. But she couldn't protect herself from Mr. Demon Lover?

"Nothing," she said flatly. "As usual. A whole lot of nothing with Angel."

Xander looked very happy as he said, in a voice dripping with commiseration, "Bummer."

Willow said, "I don't understand. He likes you. More than likes you."

"Angel barely says two words to me," Buffy told her miserably.

"Don't you hate that," Xander offered.

"And when he does, he treats me like a child," Buffy went on.

"That bastard!" Xander cried.

"You know, at least Tom can carry on a conversa-

Angel

The Slayer and her Slayerettes

"You're the Mystery Guy who appears out of nowhere, but if you *are* hanging around me, I'd like to know why."   —Buffy

"What did you think, Angel? That she would look at your true face and give you a kiss?"
—Darla

"There's mention over two hundred years ago in Ireland of Angelus, the one with the angelic face."
—Giles

"You still don't understand your part in all of this, do you? You're not the hunter . . . you're the lamb."
—The Master

David Boreanaz plays Angel, aka "Dead Boy."

tion." The thought caused her a small amount of joy. Or was she talking herself into it?

"Yeah, Tom," Xander said brightly. Then, "Who's Tom?"

"The frat guy," Willow explained.

"Oh, Buffy, I don't think so." Xander weighed the options. "Frying pan, fire. You know what I'm saying?"

In the library, Giles moved stealthily, thrust with the short sword, turned and lunged, turned and lunged, did a half-circle as he thrust again, asking "Will you be ready if a vampire is behind you?"

Then he launched the coup de grace, a sharp downward thrust into the imaginary villain's evil, unbeating heart as—

Buffy, Willow, and Xander strolled through the library's double doors.

He straightened and said, "Oh. Didn't see you three creeping about." He tossed the sword into the weapons locker. "How did it go last night?"

Buffy showed him the bracelet. "I found this."

Willow looked at it as Giles took it from her. Xander sat on the checkout counter and continued reading his magazine. Giles made a mental note that the boy had some sort of outside interest besides Buffy, and was glad of it.

Giles read the letters aloud. *"E, N, T."*

Willow ventured, "I've seen something like that before."

"It's broken in two," Buffy said. "I don't know

what the other letters might have spelled. And there's blood on it."

Her powers of observation must be keener than he credited. "Oh, I didn't see any," he offered.

"Angel"—Buffy's voice caught on the name—"showed up. He could smell it."

From his perch, Xander said, "The blood? *There's* a guy you want to party with."

"Blood," Giles said, mentally starting a list of clues. That led to what, he wondered.

"In Sunnydale." Willow flashed an expression of mock innocence. "What a surprise."

Xander closed his magazine and slid off the counter. "Okay. Here's what we're going to do. She should probably make the rounds again tonight and we should try to figure out who that bracelet belongs to."

Giles nodded at Xander's strategy. "Good idea. She'll patrol, and we'll reconvene—"

"Oh, hello," Buffy sang out, "'she's' standing right here, and she's not available."

Giles was taken aback. "Why not?"

Xander began, "Buff, this is a little more important than—"

Buffy made a little face and said, "I've got a mountain of homework to do. My mom's not really feeling well and she could probably use my help. And to be truthful, I'm not feeling all that well myself."

Giles said in a rush, "Oh, sorry. Of course if you're not well . . ."

"I'll take an early pass this evening and one later, but for the bulk of the evening . . ."

Excellent girl. Despite her illness she was not shirking her duty. Giles said generously, "You should stay with your mother."

The Three Musketeers left the library. Xander stared at Buffy, who stared back, arms folded. She said, "Well, say it."

Xander shrugged. "I'm not going to say it."

"You lied to Giles," Willow said.

Xander jabbed a finger in Willow's direction. "Because she will."

Buffy insisted, "I wasn't lying. I was protecting him from information he wouldn't be able to . . ." she grimaced, knowing how lame this was sounding, "digest properly."

"Like a corn dog," Xander zinged.

"Like you don't have a sick mother," Willow accused, "but you'd rather go to a frat party where there's going to be drinking and older boys and probably an orgy?"

Xander's eyes got big. "Whoa! Rewind! Since when did they have orgies and why aren't I on the mailing list?"

Buffy retorted, with more certainty than she felt, "There're no orgies."

Willow appeared unconvinced. "I've heard a lot of wild things go on at frat parties."

"Okay, you know what?" Buffy stopped walking. "Look. Seven days a week I'm busy saving the world. Once in a great while I want to have some fun. And that's what I'm going to have tonight. *Fun.*"

Cordelia sat across from Buffy as if she were visiting her in the big house instead of the student lounge. She said, "This isn't about fun tonight. It's about duty. *Your* duty to help me achieve permanent prosperity. Okay?" She paused a moment to let the import of the mission sink in. "Okay, dos and don'ts. Don't wear black, silk, chiffon, or Spandex. These are *my* trademarks. Don't do that weird thing to your hair."

Buffy frowned slightly. "What weird—?"

"Don't interrupt," Cordelia said. *"Do* be interested if someone should speak to you—may or may not happen. Do be polite, do laugh at appropriate intervals—" she did the weird laugh, "Ha-ha ha-ha."

Buffy thought to ask her if she'd ever seen *Amadeus* on the late show. That crusty old composer-guy, Salieri, had killed the other composer-guy, Mozart, for laughing like that.

Xander and Willow happened in. They went over to the vending machine.

"And do lie to your mother about where we're going," Cordelia continued. "It's a fraternity, and there *will* be drinking."

On that happy note, Willow and Xander wandered over. Xander said to Cordelia, "So, Cor, are you printing up business cards with your pager number and hours of operation or just going with the halter top tonight?"

"Ahh, are we a little envious?" Cordelia dished it back at him. "Don't be. You could join a fraternity of rich, powerful men. In the Bizarro world."

Buffy smiled invitingly for the Slayerettes to take a seat. "You guys want to . . . ?"

"Nah, I gotta *digest* and all," Xander drawled.

He and Willow moved away. Cordelia turned her full attention back on Buffy, tapping her fingers, thinking hard. Buffy wondered, not for the first time, what insane part of her mind she had used when she'd agreed to this.

No part. It was her hurt feelings that she'd used to think with.

"Makeup, makeup," Cordelia pondered, rubbing her chin. "Well, just give it your all and keep to the shadows." Cheerily, she closed the meeting. "We are going to have a blast!"

Buffy slammed her forehead against the table.

Willow sat with Xander a distance away. She said to him, "I can't believe she lied to Giles. My world is all askew."

"Buffy lying?" he said hotly. "Buffy going to frat parties? That's not askew, that's cockeyed!"

"Askew means cockeyed," she said kindly.

"Oh." He took their Coke from her and had a sip.

Willow took their bag of candy from him. "Well, there's nothing we can do about it. We'll help Giles—"

Xander interrupted her. "I'm going to the party."

Willow was surprised. "What?"

"I want to keep an eye on Buffy. Those frat guys creep me."

"You want to protect her." He nodded. "And you want to prove you're as good as those rich, snotty guys." He nodded again. "And maybe catch an orgy."

"If it's on early," he allowed.

She ate candy.

He drank Coke.

It was a mad scene, cars squealing up the drive, music blasting. The Delta Zeta Kappa house was enormous, and the party inside it sounded huge.

And up roared the vehicle belonging to the ambassadress from the Planet of Ambitious High School Girls: personalized plate, QUEEN C. Buffy braced herself in the passenger seat, ready for the deployment of her air bag.

Cordelia rammed the car in front of hers and said testily, "Why do they park so darn close to you?" She smiled at Buffy. "You up for this?"

They had dressed like they were up to this: Cordy in a very cool ice-blue Chinese satin dress, Buffy in black spaghetti straps and an extremely short skirt. Apparently, Buffy had not done the weird thing with her hair.

She hesitated. "I don't know. Maybe it isn't such a good idea."

"Me, too," Cordelia enthused. "Let's do it!" She plastered on her Doctor Debbi face and got out of the car.

Buffy hesitated.

"Come on," Cordelia commanded. She might as well have snapped her fingers.

They got out. Cordelia led the invasion. Buffy brought up the rear.

Buffy had always imagined that a fraternity house would be a dump, with guy stuff all over the place, posters of the Budweiser girls, that kind of thing. But the Delta Zeta Kappa house was more like the well-furnished home of a rich family. There was partying going on, that was for sure, loud music and the tinkle of ice cubes and what she supposed were typical frat touches: the waiters were apparently new frat brothers, forced to run around in their underwear or girls' underwear and full makeup, with signs around their necks that read, Pledge.

The other guys looked rich and the other girls were very pretty, no hussies need apply.

As she and Cordelia breezed in like they knew what they were doing and where they were going, a big guy with a thick neck and dark hair guzzled a huge stein of beer and looked them over with lust in his heart. He elbowed his compadre, a guy with a blond buzz job, and said, "Beaucoup babes."

"Yaaaah!" his pal agreed.

Buffy and Cordelia made it to a far corner of the room before they took stock. Buffy leaned uncomfortably against some wood paneling while Cordelia stood up straight and smiled as eagerly and sincerely as a flight attendant ready to collect boarding passes.

"You know what's so cool about college?" Cordelia told Buffy. "The diversity. You've got rich people and you've got all the other people." She perked up. "Richard!"

He of the very white teeth approached with a drink for each of them. "Welcome, ladies," he said.

"Thank you," Cordelia answered. Buffy said nothing.

Richard toasted them and drank. Cordelia did the same.

Buffy wasn't so sure about this whole deal. "Uh, is there alcohol in this?"

Richard was comforting. "Just a smidge."

"Come on, Buffy," Cordelia urged. "It's just a smidge."

"I'll just . . ." Buffy set her drink down.

"I understand," Richard said. "When I was your age, I wasn't into grown-up things, either."

Buffy looked down miserably and played with her hands.

"Have you see our multimedia room?" Richard asked.

Wearing her "really-listening, ha-ha" face, Cordelia said in one long run-on sentence, "The one with the cheery walnut paneling and the two forty-eight inch televisions on satellite feed? No. You want to show me?"

They headed off, Richard gesturing to Buffy. "What about—"

"She's happiest by herself," Cordelia replied.

Ditched, Buffy watched them go. What had she expected?

She looked around nervously, a little enviously, at all the couples. Everybody had somebody. This had so been an error in judgment.

For he is the Pink Panther, and all other panthers must bow before him.

Xander found an open window, climbed inside, and tumbled into the frat house. He bobbed up just in time to lean across a small wet bar and pluck a drink off a passing tray. Said tray was being carried by some poor schmuck charging around in his underwear and a big baby bib, with the obligatory Pledge sign around his neck. There was another one of them across the room in a black bustier forced to parade with a tray of drinks, and for what? So they could link into the old-boy network and get some dumb, meaningless job that brought in a million dollars a year?

Speaking of linking into, Xander knew he was going to pass muster in his red polo shirt and khakis. Most of the guys were wearing shirts and ties, true, but a few were natty and cazh, like him.

He grabbed a drink and joined the party, smiling at girls, smiling at food.

Alone again, still. Naturally.

Her back to the main dance area, Buffy played with her hands, turned back in the direction of her drink, picked it up, and put it back. She wished she matched the wallpaper. Not that there was wallpaper. Okay, then, she wished that her dress was a charming shade of Navajo White.

Couples danced closely together. Lots of couples. Guys and girls were meeting, smiling, talking. This party was a very lonely place to be if you were lonely.

Then, across the room, a guy who was pretty much of a honey smiled at her and raised his glass to her, looking very serious, like he thought she looked good. Cool. She picked her drink back up, did the toasting thing, and took a very small sip. Whoa. Way strong.

Then the thick-necked, dark-haired guy of "beaucoup babes" fame started making like he was going to dance all the way over to her. As she watched, wide-eyed, he got his mojo workin'. "New girl! Come on, sweetheart! Dance! Ahhhyeeahh," he yelled as he barreled toward her.

She looked left and right for a polite avenue of escape—you did not kickbox intruders into submission at frat parties, she guessed. Just as the guy was about to land on her, Tom wrapped a hand around Buffy's upper arm and pulled her out of the end zone.

"May I have this dance?" he asked.

He ushered her to the dance floor as the guy broke on through to the other side.

Then Tom pulled her into his arms, and they slow-danced.

"Thanks for—" Buffy began.

"No. We're not all a bunch of drunken louts," Tom said apologetically. "Some of us are sober louts." He smiled and glanced down shyly. "I'm

112

really glad that you decided to come." He waited a beat, then bent his knees and peered into her eyes. "And you're not."

She sighed and smiled tightly. "No. It's just . . . I shouldn't be here."

"Because you're seeing someone," he finished for her.

"No."

"You're not seeing someone?"

It was painful even to say. "Someone's not seeing me."

"So why shouldn't you be here?" he pressed.

Where to begin? "Because I have obligations, people that I'm responsible for . . . or to . . . or with." She shrugged and laughed uneasily. "It's complicated."

"You're big on responsibility. I like that. But there's such a thing as being too mature. You should relax and enjoy yourself once in a while."

Buffy looked at him curiously. "You think I'm too mature?"

He laughed at himself. "I talk too much. Have you picked up on that yet? Anyway, the Hulk is gone so you don't have to dance with me—"

He started to step back. She didn't let him go, putting his arm back around her as she said, "He might come back."

He regarded her seriously. She got a little closer, and they danced like two normal people digging on each other on a normal night at a normal party.

* * *

Xander was impressing the hell out of them. He grabbed two crab claws off a tray and waved them in the air, announcing, in his best Japanese accent, "Godzilla is attacking downtown Tokyo! Argh! Argh!"

The two babe-types laughed.

The king of comedy. Xander reigned supreme.

There were others who were not so amused. Richard stood with two of his frat brothers, a large one with dark hair and a large one with a short blond buzz job.

The dark-haired one said, "Who's this dork?"

"Never saw him before in my life," Richard drawled.

"We got us a crasher." The guy with the buzz job was delighted.

Richard smiled unpleasantly. Unpleasant things could happen to uninvited guests. And they would. He would see to that.

The three fraternity brothers moved toward Xander.

Xander asked the two hotties, "So have you seen a pair of girls here? One of them is about so high—" He measured off to the tip of Buffy's sweet blond head.

Three guys surrounded him. One of them was Cordelia's Beemer Boy. Xander said, "Hey, guys," with as much innocent pleasantry as he could muster.

One of the other guys, with dark hair and no neck, shouted, "New pledge!"

"New pledge!" said the third guy, this one with short blond hair.

They hooked their arms under his shoulders and began to drag him away. Everyone else started laughing and chanting, "New pledge!" moving in on Xander until he was lost, literally, in a crowd of rich guys with beers and attitudes.

So not a great place to be.

Buffy wandered outside to get some air. The party was happening. She was not.

Something crunched beneath her shoe.

She bent down. It was a shard of glass.

She straightened and looked up at the second story. A door was boarded over with slats that looked hastily nailed into place.

"You okay?" Tom asked, joining her.

Startled, she whirled around, dropping the piece of glass. "Yeah. I was just . . . thinking."

They were pumping up the volume inside. Richard the Smarmy strolled out, a little tipsy, and handed Buffy and Tom each a drink. He clinked their glasses with his own.

"To my Argentinean junk bonds, which just matured in double digits!"

He held up his glass and guzzled down the contents.

Tom gave Buffy a look and said, "To . . . maturity." He raised his glass.

"What the hell," Buffy said. She chug-a-lugged the whole darn thing, taking Tom by surprise. Good. "I'm tired of being mature."

Tom smiled.

So did Richard.

As usual, Willow and Giles were pulling night duty doing scary-factor research in the library. Willow didn't mind. Before Buffy came along, she had spent most of her nights doing homework, surfing the Net, or watching other, cooler people have more fun than she and Xander at the Bronze.

Willow held the bracelet Buffy had found and typed various combinations of *E, N, T* into the computer to see if anything clueful popped up.

Willow continued, "Bent."

Giles suggested, "Sent."

Willow: "Rent"

Giles: "Lent."

Willow: "Kent." Bong! Connection made. "Kent! That's it!"

Giles said, "Her boyfriend's name is Kent?"

Willow was on a roll. Her fingers flew. "No. Kent Preparatory School. Just outside town. That's where I've seen these bracelets."

Giles leaned in toward her and looked at the monitor screen. "What are you doing?"

"Pulling up their school newsletter for the last few months, to see if there's anything about—"

"A missing girl," Giles finished, as he and Willow looked together at a front page of the *Kent School News*. Above a photo of a young, pretty girl, blared the headline, CALLIE, OUR HEARTS AND PRAYERS ARE WITH YOU.

I'm doing this for Buffy, I'm doing this for Buffy, Xander thought, as he both scanned for his pal and, as an added bonus, allowed himself to be totally humiliated before a cast of at least four dozen.

The jerkwater fratboys had grabbed his head and puckered up his lips. They were smearing lipstick, in a shade that was so terribly wrong for him, all over his mouth. His shirt was gone and he was wearing a bra that would have dwarfed even Dolly Parton. He wore a gray silk skirt.

"Come on, dance, pretty boy!" said the guy with the short blond hair. Xander swayed lamely from side to side. "Come on, shake it! Don't break it!" They were swatting him with paddles, even the girls who had laughed at his Godzilla routine.

It was getting to be a bit much and he couldn't see Buffy, so he said, unsmiling, "Okay, big fun. Who's next?"

He started to walk away, but the dark-haired guy with no neck grabbed him and smashed a long, curly blond wig on his head. "You are, doll-face. Keep on dancing." He whirled him around.

The guy with the blond buzz job started twisting the night way.

"Dance, stranger," he said, laughing.

Xander danced.

I'm doing this for Buffy.

* * *

Either something was terribly wrong with her, or Buffy was a world-class lightweight when it came to drinking.

She could barely see the spinning room as it shifted and pitched. Some guy with long blond hair was dancing with his back to her in a bra and half slip.

She mumbled, "Tom?" but no one answered.

Weaving, she found some stairs and headed up them, bobbing like a cork on the ocean. Down a hall, she pushed open a door and stumbled into someone. She slurred, "Oh, sorry," then realized it was a dresser or a statue, or something. Whatever.

She looked across the room and saw a big, inviting bed. Yes. She minced across the room and climbed onto it.

"Okay. Nice bed. Just need to stop spinning for a . . ."

She lay down, completely out of it.

Richard opened the door and crept toward the sleeping girl. She lay on her side. He rolled her over onto her back and trailed his fingers across her skin.

Someone grabbed him and threw him against the wall. It was Tom, who said angrily, "Get away from her."

Richard frowned. "I wasn't doing anything."

Tom glared at him. "I *saw* what you were doing."

"I just wanted to have a little fun," Richard argued.

Tom said in a menacing voice, "Well, she's not here for your fun, you pervert! She's here for the pleasure of the One we serve."

Richard slid his glance to the side and said obediently, "In His name."

"And that goes for the other one, too," Tom ordered him.

They both turned and looked at the inert form of the little blond's friend, Richard's "date," Cordelia. She was propped between the nightstand and the bed where the blond—was her name Buffy? Did it matter?—lay unconscious.

CHAPTER 3

In the library, Giles read a printout of the *Kent School News*.

"Callie Megan Anderson . . . missing for over a week. No one's seen her, no one knows what happened to her," he said.

"This being Sunnydale and all," Willow observed, "I guess we can rule out something good."

That must have activated Giles's sense of Slayer duty, for he thought a moment, reached for the phone, and announced, "I'm calling Buffy."

"No!" Willow shouted.

He looked confused. "Why not?"

Stay calm, think fast, Willow told herself. "Because Buffy and her mother—"

"Are sick," Giles finished. "You're right. We shouldn't disturb them until we know more."

More, Willow thought. *Oh, no, not more.* "You

mean like if there are others?" Because there were, lots of others, scrolling up the screen.

"Brittany Oswald, junior at St. Michael's, disappeared a year ago. So did Kelly Percell, sophomore at Grant."

"A year," Giles said, musing, as he read over her shoulder.

"Almost to the day."

Giles's neural net was making its clever Giles connections. She could see it in his eyes. "An anniversary. Or perhaps some other event significant to the killer."

Willow ascended shrill mode. "Killer? Now there's a killer? We don't know there's a—"

"No. But this being Sunnydale and all . . ."

Her own words, back to haunt her. "Gulp."

"We need to know where Buffy found that bracelet, and then we can begin a search from there." Giles again reached for the phone.

Willow said quickly. "Good idea. Call Angel." Giles looked at her. She was working overtime; the last time she'd covered so thoroughly for anyone had been in the fifth grade, when she'd played lookout so a bunch of girls could smoke in the bathroom. Now she'd graduated to lying about frat parties. Prison was surely next. "He was there when Buffy found it. We're gonna need all the help we can get."

It must have made sense. This time she said nothing as he picked up the phone.

* * *

The party was over. The drunken stragglers were stumbling out. Xander, still attired as Sunnydale's answer to Demi Moore in one or several of her films got shown the door by his old friends, dark-haired frat boy and blond-haired frat boy. They threw him his clothes and started to shut the door.

"Party's over, jerkwater," the blond frat boy said, laughing.

Xander said, "Wait. A friend of mine was here.'

Dark-haired frat boy paused, gave him the once over. "You know, in all that light, with the wig and all"—he let the thought hang as he gave Xander a mock admiring glance—"you're still butt ugly."

He and his good buddy chortled at this most awesome display of rapier wit as they slammed the door in Xander's face. Fuming, Xander dropped his clothes onto the porch and whipped off the bra and wig.

The party *was* over.

It had served its purpose, and now it was time to fulfill the promise.

A male figure, stripped to the waist, knelt before the dark pit. His upper body was a mass of raised diamond-shaped scars. The others, robed and hooded, kept a respectful distance.

A cup and a sword rested on the edge of the pit Richard slowly carried the sword over to the kneeling figure. Holding it very formally, he began to slice into the figure's back.

The pain was cleansing; the pain was good.

In His name . . .

Cordelia had just come to. Chained to the rock wall, she was filled with fear as she looked at Buffy, who was also chained and who had been awake for some time. Buffy was taking in everything as furiously as she could: strength of bonds, possible escape routes, number of rich guys' butts to kick.

Cordelia's voice was wobbly. "Buffy, where are we?"

"In the basement, far as I can tell," Buffy replied, staying calm.

"What's happening? What did they do to us?"

"They drugged us," Buffy replied angrily. She'd been so stupid. Where was her spider sense when she needed it? Why had she pulled this prank? When would she stop being sixteen?

Maybe a little sooner than she'd expected, from the look of things.

"Why?" Cordelia demanded. "What are they going to do to us?"

"I don't know." Buffy was still looking, still assessing. It took extra effort to respond to Cordelia, but she knew she had to keep the other girl calm enough to help with their escape—if they could pull one off.

Cordelia, however, was measuring eight-point-oh on the freakout scale. She sobbed, like a little girl, "I want to go home!"

A voice from the darkness said dully, "No one's going home . . ."

It was a girl, probably once pretty, but whose hair now hung in greasy strings and whose face was chapped with lips parched. "Ever," she said, without fear, without hope.

Terrifying much?

"One of them's different from the others. Nicer,' she went on.

Buffy breathed, "Tom," at the same time she realized he was the one whose back Richard had been carving.

As if Buffy had called to him, Tom turned around and looked straight at her. Two of the hooded figures slipped a teal-green robe over his shoulders.

The girl nodded. "He's the one to watch out for."

Tom strode over to the girls as if he were the king of beasts. He gazed at Buffy for a long, creepy beat. Then he said, "She's last."

Cordelia spoke up. "Last? For what? Who's first? Answer me! Who's first?"

Tom ignored her. He walked back to the pit and emptied three stones out of a small black pouch.

"Three stones," Buffy noted. "Three of us."

"Buffy!" Cordelia pleaded.

"Stay calm," Buffy said firmly. "We'll get out of this."

Tom poured water over the stones and put them on the side of the pit.

"Why'd I ever let you talk me into coming here!" Cordelia wailed. Buffy's lips parted at Cordelia's selective memory. Well, she'd known the job was dangerous when she took it.

Only, not really.

Summoned by Giles, Angel had arrived at the library. He and the Watcher were standing in front of one of the glass windows, and Willow was staring directly into the window, agog.

Angel said, "She found the bracelet in the cemetery, near the south wall."

Willow kept staring.

Giles pondered a moment. "South wall." Then he turned to Willow and said, "What are you doing?"

Busted. Willow managed, "Oh. Sorry. The reflection thing . . . that you don't have," she said to the vampire. "Angel, how do you shave?"

She moved on. "South wall, that's near the college, and . . ." *Oh, no.*

"The fraternity house," she added, beginning to wig. The Delta Zeta Kappa fraternity house!

"A fraternity?" Giles asked.

Willow nodded wildly. She was so upset that she was experiencing a communications meltdown. No, no, no, no!

Angel put in, "Could they be taking these girls?"

Still unable to make a sound, Willow nodded.

"Let's get out there," Angel said.

The two men started to leave as Willow tried and tried and finally eeked out, "Buffy!"

Giles gave his head a little shake. "We don't know if this is concrete. Let's not disturb her until——"

"Is there," Willow confessed. "With Cordelia. They went to a party at the Zeta Kappa house!"

Giles was astounded. "She *lied* to me?"

"Oooh," Willow said, not overjoyed in her important new position as secret breaker.

"Did she . . . have a date?" Angel asked, likewise not overjoyed.

"Oooh," Willow said, then pretty much just lost it. "Why do you think she went to that party?" she demanded of Angel. "Because you gave her the brush off!"

Then she turned her epic wrath on Giles. "And you never let her do anything, except work and patrol and . . . I know she's the Chosen One, but you're killing her with the pressure. I mean, she's sixteen going on forty!"

She was mad at everybody, including life, for handing Buffy this huge, unfair plate of yucky duties and responsibilities. It was like being forced to eat every single meal in the cafeteria for the rest of your life. It was like never having hot water in your house. It was like . . .

Like waking up every morning knowing that vampires and demons were going to follow you all over the place and try to kill you unless you killed them first, and meanwhile you had to pass history and never tell your mother why you got in so much trouble all the time.

She went back to Angel, not finished with him. He

was hurting Buffy the worst. "And *you*. I mean, you're gonna live forever. You don't have time for a cup of coffee?"

Willow took a deep breath, no less surprised by her ballistic monologue than Giles and Angel.

"Okay," she said. "I don't feel better now and we gotta help Buffy."

She led the way.

They followed.

Xander carried his clothes as he stomped away from the frat house. "One day I'll have money, prestige, power," he stewed. "And on that day, they'll still have more."

Like whatever bozo owned this flashmobile, he thought angrily, glaring down at the wicked red car at the curb. Then he looked harder. The license plate read QUEEN C.

He looked around, started to move.

It was not time to leave just yet.

Stony-faced and very much in command, Tom stood on the stairs that led to the frat house main floor—and freedom—with the long sword in his hands. He said reverently, "Machida."

"In his name," the others chanted, like the monks on that CD Willow had. The monk-chanting one.

He started going down the stairs. "We who serve you, we who receive all that you bestow, call upon you in this holy hour." He walked toward the girls without looking at them.

Then he turned toward the pit. "We have no wealth, no possessions, except that which you give us."

His fellow psychotics intoned, "Except that which you give us."

He put the sword into Richard's outstretched hands. "We have no power, no place in the world, except that which you give us."

The brothers murmured again, "Except that which you give us."

Cordelia said to Buffy, "What are they, some kind of cult?"

"A psycho-cult," Buffy answered. No CD for this group.

"You've got to do something," Cordelia prodded.

"It has been a year since our last offering," Tom continued. "A year in which our bounty overflowed. We come before you with fresh offerings." He gestured toward the girls.

Uh-oh.

"Offerings," Cordelia repeated. "He's talking about *us?*"

The other girl glared at her. "Do you see anyone else chained up in here?"

"Accept our offerings, dark lord," Tom prayed. Buffy pulled on her chains. "And bless us with your power. Machida!" He extended his hand over the pit.

"Machida!" the others echoed.

One, two, three. Tom dropped the stones into the pit.

Cordelia asked shakily, "What . . . what's down there?"

"Come forth," Tom said. His arms were raised. "And let your terrible countenance look upon your servants and their humble offering! We call you, Machida!"

"In His name! Machida!"

They all knelt, Richard with the sword before him, like some knight in shining armor. Yeah, right.

Cordelia began to wig. "There's something down there. And they're going to throw us down there with it!"

Suddenly a subsonic rumbling vibrated the stones beneath Buffy's feet. It was like an earthquake as the sound began to fill the cavern.

Buffy said, "I don't think so."

Cordelia grabbed that notion and squeezed it for all it was worth. "No? Well, that's good. That's . . ."

Buffy hated to state the obvious. "I don't think we go to it. It comes to us."

The rumbling intensified. The earth shook. Something was coming. Something was escaping the pit.

For a moment, Buffy was so stunned she couldn't register what it was. She had battled many dark things, many hideous monsters. But she had never seen a thing like this. It was half man, half snake, the upper half muscular, with a man's torso and arms, but webbed, and as it examined the girls with its blank, snakelike eyes, Buffy took in its hideous, long fangs and reptilian face.

From the waist down, it was all snake, and she had no idea how long it was as it trailed into the depths of the pit.

Cordelia began shrieking. She completely and totally panicked, no passing Go. Buffy could not go there. She wanted to, but she had to try to save them.

But as she stared at the monster, she wondered if this time the Slayer had met her match.

The monster thrust out its chest and spread its arms over its followers as if to embrace them. Tom raised his arms and said, "For he shall rise from the depths and we shall tremble before him. He who is the source of all we inherit and all we possess. *Machida!*"

The others shouted, "Machida!"

Tom went on, "And if he is pleased with our offerings, then our fortunes shall increase."

The others cried, "Machida, let our fortunes increase."

"And on the tenth day of the tenth month he shall be enhungered and we shall feed him."

The monster wheeled on his long tail and examined the girls. Cordelia yelled, "Feed him? *Feed him?*"

Buffy yanked as hard as she could at her own chains as the monster swooped toward Cordelia. They held fast. Buffy kept struggling. There had to be a way out. Had to be . . .

Angel, Willow, and Giles climbed out of the Gilesmobile and headed for the darkened Delta Zeta Kappa fraternity house.

"Looks like everyone's gone," Willow said hopefully. Angel echoed her hope. Maybe Buffy and Cordelia were home, snug in their beds.

"Hey," someone said. Angel turned.

"Hi." It was Xander, dressed in a hooded black robe. He pulled the hood back and said, "What are you doing here?"

Willow said in a rush, "There's a bunch of girls missing, the Zeta Kappas may be involved, and Buffy . . ." She paused. "Are you wearing makeup?"

Xander rubbed his face. "No. I think Buffy's still inside somewhere with Cordelia." He pointed. "That's her car."

Angel began to get very worried.

Giles gestured to Xander's robe. "Why are you wearing that?"

Xander said, "Oh, I found it in their trash." He gestured toward the house. "I saw them through the windows. They were wearing robes and went to the basement. I was going to use it to sneak in."

Giles said, "They may be involved in some kind of ritual."

Angel's fear lit his impulses like a fuse.

Willow added, "With the missing girls."

Angel looked at the house, his anger mounting. "With Buffy," he said. With his Buffy. Those smug young men . . . those rich fools, who thought they could do anything to anyone. If any of them had so much as touched her, he would rip out their throats.

He felt his face change and growled deep in his throat. The others—usually so friendly—took a step back, obviously afraid of him.

"Okay," Xander said with admiration. "That *is* the guy you want to party with."

Machida rose up in all his sickly blue, leathery glory, ready for the first course: Cordelia.

Cordelia shrieked and struggled as he dove toward her.

"Hey, Reptile Boy!" Buffy shouted at him, hoping to divert his attention.

Machida turned his gaze on her.

"No woman speaks to him!" Tom commanded.

"You don't want her," Buffy said to the monster. "She's all skin and bones. Half an hour later, you'll be hungry. Why don't you try me?"

"I told you to shut up!" Tom backhanded her hard, nearly knocking her out. Then he drew the sword and angled it across her neck. "Speak again and I'll cut your throat."

Xander knocked on the door to the house. It opened.

Ah, there were his old buddies, No-Neck and Buzz Job. Xander kept his face hidden inside the robe and mumbled, "Got locked out dumping the trash. Let me in. I don't want to miss the 'you know what.'"

No-Neck was a little suspicious, but he unlatched the door and mumbled, "Come on." That was because he was one of those stupid, mean guys everybody has on his football team.

Xander flew at him and hit him as hard as he could in the face. No-Neck staggered backward as Xander said, "Where are they?" before he doubled over, grabbing his fist in pain. Then Buzz Job charged him.

Angel flew over the transom, decked Buzz Job, and moved aside so Willow and Giles could get inside.

Two of the robed guys unchained Cordelia and held her as she fought them in a frenzy.

From above, the sounds of fighting and crashing alerted Tom, who said, "Something's going on upstairs. Go. Go!" to several of the hooded figures. They dashed up the stairs. Tom said to Machida, "Feed, dark lord."

Cordelia thrashed and screamed as the hooded figures clutched her.

Machida dove at her.

She screamed and screamed as the creature grabbed her; and while it appeared that all hell was breaking lose, Buffy broke lose, too. With every ounce of her strength, she ripped her chains right out of the wall. As Machida gripped Cordelia and opened wide for the first delectable bite, Buffy smashed him in the head. He dipped forward, then reared back against the wall of the pit, growling.

The two hooded Zetas released Cordelia, who darted out of the way as Buffy kicked one in the head, then spun and took out the other one with a back kick.

In a rage, Tom picked up the long sword and charged her. She ducked and backed away just in time as the razor-sharp blade nearly took off her head.

Upstairs, the Zetas met the cavalry.

Angel threw a robed guy to the floor. Willow jumped over the guy's body and headed for the cellar door, disappearing inside. Xander rode No-Neck piggyback, and hit the guy on the head over and over and over.

"That's for the wig," he said. *Wham.* "That's for the bra." *Wham.*

Giles rattled another door. A Zeta charged him. Giles straightened and decked him, looking mildly pleased with himself.

Willow flew back out through the cellar door and shouted, "Some guy's attacking Buffy with a sword!" Then she processed what she'd just seen downstairs and added, "Also, there's a really big snake."

Xander was riding some guy like a bucking bronco, smashing him over the head, and saying, "That's for the makeup and that's for the last sixteen and a half years!"

Xander gave the guy one last good wallop and leaped off. The guy fell forward. Willow winced as he crashed right onto his face.

Angel decked two more guys. Willow realized her menfolk hadn't heard her and tried again.

"Guys, Buffy, snake, basement, *now!*"

Everyone got it that time. They charged the basement door.

Angel smashed one more face in on his way downstairs.

It's just a battle like any other, Buffy told herself. But it wasn't. There were more bad guys than usual. And one of them was a lot bigger, too.

She scrambled away from Tom as he smashed the sword into the ground.

"You . . ." he said dangerously. "I'll serve you to him in pieces."

He swung hard. Buffy ducked and countered with the chain from the wall, wrapping it around his neck. His eyes went wide with surprise and pain.

"Tom," she said, "you talk too much." She gave him a rockin' roundhouse punch and he flew across the room, demolishing a table with candles and stuff on it.

Then she registered that Angel, Willow, Xander, and Giles were tearing downstairs as Machida made another concerted effort to devour Cordelia.

"Helllllppppp!" Cordelia shrieked.

Buffy jumped up on the ledge of the pit with the sword and swung at Machida. "Back off, wormy!" she shouted.

The monster growled. She brought the sword down hard and fast in the middle of its body, hacking it in two.

It was over.

Giles ran to collect Cordelia. Willow and Xander hurried off to the other girl who was being held captive. Buffy stood alone.

Filled with emotion, Cordelia wailed, "You did it. You saved us."

She walked right past Buffy and sank into Angel's arms. Angel looked hard at Buffy, who looked down. Okay. He didn't love her. That was okay. She didn't care. She had nearly died; what did he matter in the Slaying scheme of things?

Cordelia went on, "I've never been so happy to see anyone in my whole . . ." She fought back tears as Angel moved away from her and went to collect Tom. "You guys," she said, "I really . . . hate you guys. The weirdest things always happen around you."

Willow and Xander helped the other girl up the stairs. As Tom walked past with Angel, Cordelia whirled on him. "You're going to jail for about fifteen thousand years."

Tom glared at her and went up the stairs, Angel following closely behind.

Giles stood alone with Buffy. Buffy made her little pout face—the one that did not affect him, ever, no matter how glad he was to see her alive—and said, "I told one lie. I had one drink."

"Yes, and you nearly got devoured by a giant demon-snake," he shot back. "The words *let that be a lesson* are a tad redundant at this juncture."

"I'm sorry."

He could tell she meant it. He gave ground. "So am I." His grave sense of responsibility compelled him to add, "I drive you too hard because I know what you have to face. From now on," he promised, "no more pushing, no more prodding." He paused, continued. "Just an extraordinary amount of nudging."

Arm in arm, Slayer and Watcher left the pit.

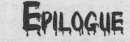

EPILOGUE

It was the Bronze. It was night.

It was a short, eager freshman, who said, "C'mon, c'mon," to the coffee-making person as the cappuccino machine fizzed and spit. "Hurry up."

Then everything was ready, and he scurried off, bearing gifts—a frothy cup and a plate with a muffin on it—to Queen Cordelia, who looked at him with utter disdain.

"Thank you, Jonathon," she said, giving him the regal eye. "Did we forget something?"

He glanced down worriedly, and muttered, "Cinnamon, chocolate, half-caff, non-fat." Then it came to him: "Extra foam!"

She plucked the muffin off the plate and gave him a series of well-go-get-it flicks of her hand. He whisked the coffee away.

Cordelia walked over to the table where Willow,

Buffy, and Xander sat. Xander was reading the *Sunnydale Press*.

"Young men," Cordelia drawled. "The only way to go." She strolled off.

Xander told the others, "It says here they'll all get consecutive life sentences. Investigators found bones of the missing girls in a huge cavern beneath the frat house, and older bones dating back fifty years."

Xander continued reading. "A surprising number of corporations whose chairmen and founders are former Delta Zeta Kappas are suffering falling profits, IRS raids, and suicides in the board room." He quipped, "Starve a snake, lose a fortune. Well, I guess the rich really are different, huh."

Willow said to Buffy, "Have you heard from Angel?"

Buffy shook her head. She almost added, *Of course not.*

Willow leaned toward her intently. "When he got so mad about you being in danger and changed into . . . *grrrr,*" she flashed an expression of intense vampire anger as interpreted by a mild-mannered compubrain, "it was the most amazing thing I ever saw. I mean, how many guys can—"

Xander frowned as he kept reading the paper. Then he looked at Willow. "Angel, Angel, Angel. Does every conversation always have to come around to that freak?"

Emerging from the shadows, Angel walked up to the table. Buffy's heart skipped a beat. Xander said, "Hey, man, how ya doin'?" without a trace of embarrassment that Angel had heard him.

Angel looked at Buffy. "Buffy," he said.

She took a breath. "Angel."

"Xander," Xander said sarcastically, maybe hiding a little bit of hurt feelings. Maybe not. Buffy wasn't sure there was much hiding going on.

Angel looked straight at her, and she tingled down to the soles of her feet. "I hear this place serves coffee."

Coffee . . .

"Thought maybe you and I should get some."

He was asking her on a date!

She didn't respond. She would make him say it, all of it. She would make him eat his words.

"Sometime," he added.

She still kept her face a mask.

"If you want," he finished.

And with the tingling came the triumph. Okay, maybe she was a freak who staked vampires when everybody else was gabbing on the phone about their boyfriends. Maybe she was a mess half the time he saw her, from punching out demons and fighting the forces of darkness. Maybe she would never be homecoming queen in this town.

But *Angel* wanted to have *coffee* with *her.*

"Yeah," she said, savoring the sweet, sweet moment.

Angel brightened. He looked happy—and relieved.

"Sometime," she went on. "I'll let you know."

She got up, slid off her stool, and started walking.

Willow looked at Angel and Xander. They both wore slightly amazed expressions tinged with respect. She liked that. Respect was good. Buffy deserved it. A lot of it.

He asked me out, Buffy thought. *He wants to date me.*

She walked on into the night, head high.

Her smile grew.

THE THIRD CHRONICLE:

Lie to Me

Prologue

Playgrounds at night are lonely places. Children should not be left in them.

Bad things can happen.

Awash in eerie moonglow, the little merry-go-round turned slowly. The swings rocked, as if gently pushed by the night wind.

Eight-year-old James sat inside the jungle gym and looked out over the park for his family's minivan. At home, it was warm and cozy; his older sister was probably catching up on her *Melrose Place* reruns while something good cooked for dinner.

"Come on, Mom," he said, half-angry, half-anxious. "She's always late." She was always after him to be home by dark. But when she was supposed to pick him up, where was she?

"Are you lost?" asked a voice.

James turned, startled but not scared. It was a

very pretty lady in a long white dress. Her skin was almost as white as her dress. She had a funny smile on her lips and she seemed to have trouble walking. James wondered if she was hurt.

"No, my mom's just supposed to pick me up, is all," he told her, climbing out of the jungle gym to face her.

"Do you want me to walk you home?" She talked funny, too. Like the bad guys on the cartoons.

"No, thank you," he said politely.

The lady walked closer to the jungle gym and started slowly around, running her long, white fingers along the bars. Now she was a little closer, and now James was just a little bit nervous.

He walked around the other way. Her eyes looked funny. Like she wasn't really seeing him.

"My mummy used to sing me to sleep at night. 'Run and catch, run and catch, the lamb is caught in the blackberry patch.' She had the sweetest voice." She closed her eyes and smiled.

Okay, now he was getting scared. Now he was starting to figure out that this lady was maybe kind of cuckoo, running around in what looked like her nightgown with no sweater and not minding the cold.

And now she was staring at him. "What will your mummy sing when they find your body?"

He didn't understand what she meant, but he understood that he should do something to protect himself. He began to inch away from her. "I'm not supposed to talk to people," he told her.

She looked at him like you do when you watch someone eat something you really want. "Well, I'm not a person, see," she began, coming toward him as he kept moving away, "so that's just—"

A dark figure stepped between James and the lady. James jerked back, looking up to see the face of a man. The man looked so angry he almost frightened James worse than the lady.

So when he said, "Run home," James did. As fast as his legs could go.

And he never played in that park again.

Angel made sure the boy was safe. Then he took a moment before he turned to face the child's attacker.

As he did, her pale face lit up. He had known it would. And he hated himself for it.

"My Angel," she said in her breathy, singsong voice. The voice of madness.

"Hello, Drusilla." He felt no similar joy on seeing her. Only guilt and the perpetual remorse that, thanks to the Romani curse, haunted his nights and plagued his days.

She and Spike had burst upon Sunnydale a few months before. He wasn't certain what had drawn them here. Both had personal scores to settle with him, Angel, but it was clear they had moved in for the long haul. After Buffy had killed the Master the previous spring, the vampires turned to the Anointed One as their leader. But Spike had shoved the demonic little boy into a wire cage and allowed the daylight to burn him to a cinder.

Drusilla glided slowly toward him, a sad, starved wraith. She looked very ill. "Do you remember the song Mummy used to sing me? Pretty."

He could not meet her gaze . "I remember," Angel said, his tone flat and low as all the awful images ran through his mind.

"Yes. You do," she said pointedly, and he was certain her mind was filled with their joined past as well.

"Drusilla, leave here." He looked at her hard, wanting very badly for her to listen to him. "I'm offering you that chance. Take Spike and get out."

"Or you'll hurt me?" She was not afraid.

He looked down again. He hated seeing her like this. Hated seeing what she had become.

"No. No, you can't. Not anymore." A whisper of a smile crossed her face. Did she mean that he was incapable of hurting her now that he had gotten back his soul, or that the wounds he had inflicted on her ran so deep she could not be hurt worse?

"If you don't leave," he said, "it'll go badly. For all of us."

"My dear boy's gone all away, hasn't he? To her." She was mournful.

"Who?" Angel asked, wary, alert.

It was a wet night. Rainwater glistened between the illuminated plastic skylights that bulged like loaves of bread on the rooftop where Buffy patrolled.

"The girl. The Slayer," Drusilla said. "Your heart stinks of her." She put her hand on Angel's chest, caressing him. "Poor little thing. She has no idea what's in store."

Buffy came to the edge of the roof and peered down over a playground. Hunting ground, more like. Vampires congregated here—

She froze.

Angel was standing with a pretty girl with long, black hair. Though his back was to Buffy, she would recognize Angel's dark hair and well-cut jacket anywhere. The girl wore a long, white dress, and she was in his arms. Buffy watched, shocked. Were they kissing?

"This can't go on, Drusilla," Angel said. "It's got to end."

"Oh, no, my pet." She leaned in close, as if taking in his essence. In Angel's ear, she whispered, "This is just the beginning."

She drifted back into the night.

With fierce sorrow, he watched her go.

So did Buffy.

Near tears.

CHAPTER 1

Another morning and Sunnydale was still on the map.

Another morning at Sunnydale High, and not only was Giles still alive and researching, but he was also accompanying Jenny Calendar, resident computer science teacher and techno-pagan, down the stairs.

"It's a secret," she was saying.

Giles pressed, "What kind of secret?"

"The kind that's secret. You know, where I don't actually tell you what it is." She grinned at him. He knew she found him highly amusing. As Xander Harris might put it, that was a plus.

He was not to be put off. "I just think it's customary that when two people are going out for an evening, that they both have an idea what they're doing."

They reached the bottom of the stairs and turned

right. He was on his way to the library, and she to the lair of that dread horde of demonic machines known as computers.

"Oh, come on!" she chided him gently. "Where's your sense of adventure?"

He tried another tack. "But, I . . . how will I know what to wear?"

She wryly took in his appearance. "Do you own anything else?"

"Not as such," he admitted.

She chuckled. "Rupert, you're going to have to trust me."

"All right." He surrendered. "I put myself in your hands."

She walked past him with a teasing smile on her face. "*That* sounds like fun." Grinning, she turned as she walked away not to the computer laboratory but to one of the exit doors. "Okay. Seven-thirty, tomorrow night?"

He was still processing the comment about her hands and fun with a pleased expression on his face. "Yes."

Buffy waited a beat as Giles and Ms. Calendar finished their goo-goo eyes session. *Some* people were doing well in the romance department. That was nice. For Giles, especially nice.

She came up to him and said, "Hey."

They began to walk together toward the library. He asked her, "Did we hunt last night?"

"I did a couple of quick sweeps downtown."

"Any encounters?"

She hesitated. There was no need to tell him, was there? Angel meeting girls on the sly had nothing to do with the forces of darkness. Uncomfortable, she said, "Nothing vampiry."

"Well, I've been researching your friend Spike. The profile is fairly unappetizing. But I still haven't got a bead on why he's here."

Buffy could barely keep her mind on the conversation. Spike. Right. Major bad vampire, new in town. She kept seeing Angel with that girl. She said, "You'll figure it out."

"Are you all right?" Giles peered at her. "You seem a little glum."

"I'm fine."

He was clearly not convinced. "Well, why don't you take the night off?"

"Oh, that'd be nice," she told him sincerely.

They were at the library with its porthole windows. Giles brightened as if happy to please her. "Yes. You could spend some time with Angel."

That hurt. Of course, Giles didn't know it hurt. "I don't know," Buffy said, downcast. "He might have other plans."

Sadly, she walked away.

In history, they were apparently discussing the French Revolution, but Buffy barely listened.

"Well, it seems like Louis XVI was just sort of a weak king," someone said.

The teacher responded, "Well, that's fair enough. Any other impressions?"

Buffy unfolded Willow's note and read, *Do you know who she was?*

In the row ahead of them, Xander sat next to Cordelia, who was actually participating.

"I just don't see why everyone is always picking on Marie Antoinette," Cordelia said. "I can *so* relate to her. She worked really hard to look that good. And people just don't appreciate that kind of effort."

Xander looked at her with his wry Xander polite stare.

Buffy wrote, *No. Dark hair. Old dress. Pretty.* She folded the note and handed it back to Willow.

Cordelia was still busily defending the French monarchy, based on its fashion sense. "And I know, the peasants were all depressed."

Xander offered, "I think you mean, 'oppressed.'"

"Whatever." Clearly she didn't want to be interrupted or corrected. "They were cranky. So they're like, 'Let's lose some heads.' That's *fair?* And Marie Antoinette cared about them. She was going to let them have cake!"

Their teacher said politely as Xander stared, "Yes, well, that's a very interesting perspective."

Willow scribbled on the note and handed it back to Buffy. Buffy opened it.

Vampire?

The bell rang. Everyone rose and gathered their books. Buffy turned to Willow as they walked into the hall and said, "I don't know. I don't think so. They seemed pretty friendly."

Xander caught up with them, ready for gossip. "Who's friendly?"

"No one," Buffy replied.

"Angel and a girl," Willow filled in.

"Will, do we have to be in total share mode?" Buffy asked, giving her a look.

"Hey, it's *me*," Xander reminded her. "If Angel's doing something wrong I need to know." He smiled. "'Cause it gives me a happy."

"I'm glad someone has a happy," Buffy said, not happily.

They walked into the lounge, hallowed hall of studying and extreme conversing.

"Aw, you just need cheering up. And I know just the thing." He hummed some funky music as he pumped his arms and swiveled his hips. "Crazed dance party at the Bronze!"

Buffy sighed. "I don't know."

Xander restrained himself with a few sways. "Very calm dance party at the Bronze."

He sat next to Willow in a chair. "Moping at the Bronze."

Someone said behind Buffy, "I'd suggest a box of Oreos dunked in apple juice, but maybe she's over that phase."

She'd know that voice anywhere. Buffy whirled around. "Ford?" She threw her arms around the tall, dark-haired boy. "Ford!"

He hugged her back. "Hey, Summers, how you been?"

This was neat. "What are you doing here?"

"Matriculating."

She had no idea what he meant. "Huh?"

"I'm finishing out my senior year at Sunnydale High. Dad got transferred."

"This is great," Buffy said, getting a happy of her own.

Ford looked kind of shy. She remembered his long bangs and his angular face. They used to joke that he looked like the hero of a dozen Japanese *anime* cartoons. "I'm glad you think so. I wasn't sure you'd remember me."

"Remember you? Duh, we were in school together for seven years. You were my giant fifth-grade crush."

"So. You two know each other?" Xander cut in.

"Oh!" Buffy looked at her two friends. Holding Ford's hand, she led him to the chairs where her two best friends—correction, best friends from *Sunnydale*—sat waiting to be introduced, and said, "I'm sorry. This is Ford. Uh, Billy Fordham. This is Xander and Willow." She pointed at them in turn.

"Hi," Xander said with one of his polite, fake smiles that sometimes accompanied Cordelia's history rambles.

"Hey," Ford replied.

"Nice to meet you." Willow smiled very sweetly.

"Ford and I went to Hemery together, in L.A." Buffy smiled at Ford bigtime. "And now you're here? For real?"

"Dad got the transfer, and boom. He just dragged me out of Hemery and put me down here."

"This is great!" She gazed up at him, remembering more normal days. Fifth grade had been way before she'd known she was the Slayer. Before her parents started fighting and eventually split up. He was a symbol of all that, and it made her feel warm inside to have him standing next to her. "Well, I mean, it's hard—sudden move, all your friends, delicate time, very emotional—but let's talk about me: this is great!"

Willow said, "So you two were sweeties in the fifth grade?"

"Not even," Buffy told her. She looked at him slyly. "Ford wouldn't give me the time of day."

"Well, I was a manly sixth grader," Ford explained. "I couldn't be bothered with someone that young."

Buffy said brightly, "It was terrible. I moped over you for months. Sitting in my room listening to that Divinyl's song, 'I Touch Myself.'"

Ooops. She ticked her glance over to Willow and Xander, then to Ford. "Of course, I had no idea what it was about."

Ford scratched his cheek and Xander gave a we-knew-that wave and politely waited for her to move on. Willow just sat there.

Move on Buffy did. "Hey," she said to Ford, "are you busy tonight? We're going to the Bronze. It's the local club and you have to come."

"I'd love to," Ford said. "But if you guys already had plans . . . would I be imposing?"

"Only in the literal sense," Xander assured him.

"Okay then." He sounded very pleased. "I gotta find the admissions office, get my papers in order."

Buffy said, "Well, I'll take you there." To Willow and Xander, she said, "See you guys in French."

"Good meeting you," Ford said. Buffy's friends returned the compliment.

Was this turning into a better day or what?

There was no joy in Xanderville. He watched Buffy glom on to the new/old boy with the happy face his own personal bag of tricks had failed to provide her.

"This is Ford, my bestest friend of all my friends," he mimicked Buffy. "Jeez. Doesn't she know any fat guys?"

Meanwhile, Willow was staring off into space, until she kind of activated, looked very startled, and said, "Oh. *That's* what that song's about?"

Bank shot!

Or something. As the music rocked and the usual suspects danced the night away, the eight ball dropped into the pocket of the pool table.

"Ford, you made it," Buffy said, joining the Slayerettes plus one. And the one was already lining up his next shot while Xander anxiously chalked up the tip of his cue.

Ford smiled at Buffy. "It wasn't hard to find."

Willow said, "Buffy, Ford was just telling us about the ninth-grade beauty contest." She smiled. "And the, uh, swimsuit competition."

Buffy frowned in mock seriousness, even though it was a pretty embarrassing story. "Oh, God, Ford. Stop that. The more people you tell about it, the more people I have to kill."

Ford hit the nearest ball with his cue. "You can't touch me, Summers. I know all your darkest secrets."

Xander drawled, "Care to make a small wager on that?"

Buffy shot a warning look from Xander to Ford and said, "I'm gonna go grab a drink. Ford, try not to talk."

Buffy walked to the bar. As she arrived, the man in front of her turned to go, drink in hand. It was Angel.

Buffy said in a low voice, "Oh."

He brightened at the sight of her. "Hey. I was hoping you'd show."

He looked good, in a dark shirt with thick designs. It looked old-fashioned, like the girl's dress. Buffy wondered if Angel liked what she herself had on: all black, dressed to kill, but not to Slay.

"You drink," she noted, surprised, indicating his coffee cup. "I mean, drinks. Non-blood things."

He replied with a flirtatious smile—or the closest thing to a flirtatious smile he had ever flashed on her, "There's a lot about me you don't know."

Her face fell as she said coolly, "I believe that."

Ford looked over at Angel with Buffy as Willow and Xander checked him out. Willow said helpfully, "That's Angel."

"He's Buffy's beau," Xander added, clearly hoping this was disappointing data for Ford. "Her special friend."

Ford studied him. "He's not in school, right? He looks older than her."

Xander said archly, "You're not wrong."

Buffy looked up into Angel's face and asked the question she did not really want to ask, but knew she had to. "So, what'd you do last night?"

He shrugged. "Nothing."

She hadn't wanted to ask because she hadn't wanted to know if Angel could, and would, lie to her. So she pressed, "Nothing at all? You ceased to exist?"

"No, I mean I stayed in. Read." He frowned slightly, as if confused by her line of questioning.

"Oh." So he was lying to her, and he was good at it, too. If she hadn't seen him "reading" last night, she would believe every word, every flicker of his expression. What had she expected from a guy who could keep secret from the Slayer that he was a vampire?

Angel kept peering down at her. She knew he knew something was up with her.

She walked back to the group. She really didn't want to go into it right then.

If ever.

Buffy rejoined her friends at the pool table, aware that Angel was trailing behind her.

Ford asked, "Didn't want that soda after all?"

"Not thirsty," she said uncomfortably.

"Hey, Angel," Willow greeted him. Buffy looked down, away, anywhere but at her vampire boyfriend.

"Hi," Ford said.

Now she was forced into hostess mode, and she tried to make the best of it. "This is Ford. We went to school together in L.A."

The two guys shook. Ford's eyes widened. "Whoa. Cold hands."

Xander drawled, "You're not wrong."

Angel's face was a mask as he regarded Ford. "So, you're here visiting Buffy?"

"No. I'm actually here to stay," Ford replied. "Just moved down." They were facing off. Buffy had to admit that Ford pretty much held his own against the older, suaver guy. Her older, suaver, two-timing guy.

Perhaps to smoothe things over, as she often did, Willow gestured to the pool table and asked, "Angel, do you want to play?"

"You know, it's getting really crowded in here tonight," Buffy blurted. "I'm a little hot." She looked at Ford, deliberately excluding Angel. "Do you want to go for a walk?"

"Uh, sure," Ford said. "That'd be nice."

Buffy looked first at Angel, then at the Slayerettes. She murmured, "See you tomorrow."

She and Ford peeled off. Angel stood stonily as they passed him.

"Good night," he said stiffly.

"Take care," Ford answered.

An awkward silence followed the awkward scene.

Xander piped up, "O-kay. Once more, with tension."

Angel's eyes narrowed. "He just moved here?"

Xander lined up a shot. "Yeah. And, boy, does he move fast." *Zing!*

Angel looked pained.

"Well, Angel," Willow ventured, "you could still play with us." But he had vanished. She didn't know how he did it. She said to Xander, "See? You made him do that thing where he's gone."

Buffy wondered what Angel thought of her grand exit as she walked along with Ford. Was he hurt? Did he care beyond the male-ego thing of caring?

"So, that was your boyfriend?" Ford asked innocently.

"No," she said, then reconsidered. "Well, yeah. Maybe." She gave a little laugh. "Could we lay off the tough questions for a while?"

Ford shrugged. "Sorry. So, what else do you do for fun around here?"

As he was speaking, Buffy heard the sounds of a scuffle around the corner. Time to think fast. Superman would look for a phone booth. And she?

"Um, uh, my purse!" she cried. "I left my purse at the Bronze. Could you get it for me? Thanks!"

"Uh, okay," Ford said.

"Good. Run. Thanks."

Taking off at a trot, he left to do she asked. As soon as his back was turned Buffy raced around the corner.

Intrigued by Buffy's behavior, Ford stopped walking toward the Bronze and turned around. He started moving slowly toward the alley. A girl raced past him, sobbing with terror. Ford glanced at her, then inched closer to the corner, more intrigued than ever.

Sounds of fighting broke the stillness of the night. A trash can lid sailed through the air like a Frisbee.

Ford turned the corner.

It was not a very good vampire. Stupid, slow, and easy to hit. However, it wasn't all that easy to tire. Finally she threw it against the wall and staked it. There was that moment where it shrieked and held its shape in dust, then exploded.

She whirled around and headed back to the Bronze. Talk about your awkward interruptions. All she needed now—

Was what she had. Ford was staring at her.

"Oh, you're back," she said awkwardly.

"What's going on?" he asked.

Thinking on her feet after a battle was not her strong point. She blurted, "There was a cat." Yeah, right. He was going to believe that in a million years. Still, she had to finish what she had started. Keeping her eyes big and innocent, she spun her very bad web. "A cat, here, and then there was, another cat. And they fought, the cats, and then they left." It was a not-good lie delivered in a not-good way. Maybe she should be proud that she was so honest.

Ford said simply, "Oh. I thought you were just slaying a vampire."

Her eyes, still wide for her cat routine, bulged. "What? Whating a what?"

Ford smiled at her. "I know, Buffy. You don't have to lie. I've been trying to figure out the right time to tell you. I know you're the Slayer."

Willow lay on her bed with her stuffed animals, wearing her bunny slippers, talking with Buffy on the phone. She said, "Just like that? He told you?"

Buffy's voice sounded very up. "Just like that. Said he found out right before I got booted from Hemery."

"Wow. It's neat." Willow paused. "Is it neat?"

At her end of the line, Buffy smiled. She said, "Yeah, I guess it is. I won't have to worry that he's going to find out my dark secret. It just makes everything easier."

In the dark, Ford walked cheerfully along the highways and byways of warehouses and other assorted rundown buildings. When he got to a particularly dilapidated structure, he pounded on the large metal door. Above the door was a painted sign: no words, just a picture of a setting sun.

A little window in the center slid open. The doorman peered out at him, saw who it was, and slid the window shut

The door opened.

Ford walked through to door number two. He patted the arm of the black-lipped guy who was welding the door hinges, propane torch hissing, sparks flying. Yeah, there'd be plenty more sparks where those came from.

Then Ford entered another world, the world of the Sunset Club. He stood on a balcony lined in blue neon, which cast an eerie, sickly glow on the club's patrons. It was the way they liked it. Below him, couples danced to ethereal music and dreamed of other, darker worlds. They wore black roses and lace, ruffled shirts and capes and, if they could have afforded them, would have slept in satin-lined coffins. The tablecloths were deep, blood red, and everyone drank from goblets. He knew what they were thinking: if only their lives could really be like this . . .

He started down the stairs. As he reached the bottom, he was accosted by none other than Marvin, the nerdiest vampire wannabe who ever walked in sunlight. He wore a ruffled shirt and a sparkly blue cape that only added to the total pathetosity of his being. No Tom Cruise, this. No Brad Pitt. Marvin he was, and Marvin he would always be.

"Ford? Hi, Ford," Marvin said edgily.

"Hey," Ford replied, wishing—not for the first time—that he had someone else to deal with.

"Well? How did it go?" Marvin was all aflutter, like some girl. Ford could hardly stand to be around him.

"Went good," Ford replied dismissively.

"Good? That's it? That's all? Well, when are we—"

"Soon," Ford assured him. And that, at least, was the truth.

But Marvin was rattled. He said, "Oh, *soon*. Oh, okay." He huffed. "You know, you could give me a little more information here. I'm trusting you. I'm out on a limb here—not to mention the lease is almost up on this place. Who's going to cover that?"

"Marvin," Ford cut in, eager to staunch the flow.

"Diego," Marvin corrected him, looking around to make sure no one else had heard the name that must not be spoken. "Come on, it's Diego now."

Ford had nearly forgotten. Marvin had changed his name to something more sinister, more romantic. "Diego, Ridalin," he advised his hyper friend. "Everything's going to be fine."

A slinky blond in a long, black, lowcut dress with white, white makeup and crimson lipstick glided up to Diego and Ford with a couple of goblets. Her name had once been Joan, but like Marvin, she had adopted a new persona. Now she was Chantarelle. Ford took one of the goblets, popped open his prescription bottle, and washed down a pill. He continued, "Just make sure you're ready when I say." He smiled at Chantarelle.

She smiled back, nervous but excited. "I can't wait."

"Well, I still think I should be in on the plan," Diego grumbled.

"Diego, you gotta trust me," Ford said, glancing past him to the video monitors hung in strategic places throughout the club. Jack Palance was playing Dracula on the video monitors around the room. Ford stared at the one behind Marvin as he sipped from his goblet. He knew every line, every gesture.

He knew the lifestyle.

He knew the promise.

He went on, soothing his front man, "A couple more days and we'll get to do the two things every American teen should have the chance to do. Die young"—he smiled at Diego and Chantarelle—"and stay pretty."

Then he lost himself in the movie, speaking every syllable just as Dracula himself spoke them, for it wasn't really a movie, was it? More like a documentary:

"So, you play your wits against mine. Me, who commanded armies hundreds of years before you were born. Fools!"

CHAPTER 2

Willow's bedtime ritual was nearly complete: a swift face wash, followed by astringent for potential zits, then teeth, and now, her long hair. She had to comb it out every night.

Someone was standing outside her French door. Nervously, she peered through her venetian blinds.

"Oh!" she cried, stunned. "Angel." She opened her door making sure there were no parent noises nearby. "What are you doing here?"

"I wanted to talk to you." He looked very serious and somewhat unhappy.

"Oh." She pulled the door all the way open and waited for him to enter. He didn't move. "Well?"

"I can't. Unless you invite me, I can't come in."

Caught off guard—never in a million years would Willow have guessed that Angel would one day see her in her nightshirt and fuzzy bunny slippers—she replied sincerely, "Oh. Okay. Uh, I invite you. To come in."

He stepped over the threshold. Willow turned toward her bed. Oh, *no!* Her bra was lying on her bedspread for all the world—and all the vampires in her room—to see. Hastily she stuffed it under her pillow.

Angel said, "If this is a bad time . . ."

"No, I just . . ." She cast an anxious glance at the door to the hallway. It was ajar. "I'm not supposed to have boys in my room." And she hadn't, ever. It was just her luck that the first one was her best friend's vampire boyfriend.

"Well," Angel said, with the hint of a smile, "I promise to behave myself."

"Okay," she said, nodding her head. "Good."

He sighed. "I guess I need help."

"Help?" She brightened, eager to have something to do besides stand there in her bunny slippers. "You mean like on homework?" She rethought. "No, because you're old and you already know stuff."

"I want you to track someone down," he told her. "On the Net." He gestured with his head toward her computer.

"Oh!" Even better than helping with homework. "Great! I'm *so* the Net girl."

She crossed to her desk, sat down, and booted up.

"I just want to find everything I can. Records, affiliates. I'm not even sure what I'm looking for yet."

She was already in the zone. Poising her hands

over the keyboard like one of the Hansons, she said, "What's the name?"

"Billy Fordham," he replied shortly.

She stopped. Then typing, she ventured, "Uh, Angel, if I say something you really don't want to hear, do you promise not to bite me?"

Wow, was he pale. He glowered down on her with his dark, dark eyes and said, with not much joy, "Are you going to tell me that I'm jealous?"

This conversation was making her nervous. "Well, you do sometimes get that way."

He thought for a moment. Then he said, "You know, I never used to."

He sat on her bed. "Things used to be pretty simple. A hundred years just hanging out, feeling guilty." He almost smiled. "I really honed my brooding skills. Then she comes along." The look on his face was the kind of needing, wanting, haunted, hungry, brooding one that you read about in romance novels. Not that she ever did, but maybe if she had, she would have known what the Divinyls song was about.

He nodded. "Yeah, I get jealous. But I know people and my gut tells me this is a wrong guy."

"Okay." That was enough for her. She trusted Angel's gut. So she continued her search. "But if there isn't anything weird . . . hey, that's weird."

Angel rose from her bed and stood behind her, looking at the screen. "What?"

"I just checked the school records and he's not in them. I mean, usually they transfer your grades and stuff. But he's not even registered."

Now a little concerned, she typed faster.

Angel said, "He said he was in school with you guys, right?"

"Let me see if I can—"

From the hall, Willow's mom called, "Willow? Are you still up?"

Willow freaked. "Ack! Go!"

Angel glided to the French door, still inside her room. She called, "I'm just going to bed now, Mom."

To Angel she murmured, "Come by at sunset tomorrow. I'll keep looking."

He nodded. Then he added, "Don't tell Buffy what we're doing, all right?"

Willow wasn't happy. "You want me to lie to her? It's Buffy."

"Just don't bring it up," Angel pressed. "Till we know what's what."

"Okay." That wasn't lying. Exactly. "It's probably nothing."

Angel said sincerely, "That'd be nice."

It was Ford's second day at school. It was great to have him there, and even more great that Buffy didn't have to hide from him who she really was and what she really did.

And there was her dear friend, Willow, getting a drink at the water fountain. "Will!" Buffy called. "What's up?"

Willow jerked ramrod straight, choking slightly as she squeaked, "Nothing."

Whoa, jumpy. Buffy said, "Do you want to hang? We're cafeteria bound."

Willow's eyes skittered right, left. She said, in a jerking, stilted tone, "I'm going to work in the computer lab. On school work that I have. So I cannot hang just now." She glanced at Ford. "Hi, Ford."

"Morning," he replied in his friendly way.

Buffy eyed her best friend. "Okay, Will. Fess up."

Willow had that headlight/deer thing going. "What?"

"Are you drinking coffee again?" Buffy asked in her best mom voice. "Because we talked about this."

Willow burst out in a peal of semi-maniacal laughter. As if she needed to elaborate, she explained to Ford, "It makes me jumpy." Then to both Buffy and Ford, she said, "I have to go. Away." And off she fled.

Ford said, "Nice girl."

"There aren't two of those in the world," Buffy said, chuckling. She was definitely going to have to talk to Will about decaf.

Then Giles walked up. He looked at Ford, then at Buffy, and said, "Buffy. Ms. Calendar and I are going . . . somewhere . . . tonight. She's given me the number of her beeper thingy in case you need me for"—again he glanced at Ford—"study help. Suddenly."

Buffy lowered her voice and leaned toward her Watcher. "He knows, Giles."

Giles was clearly taken aback. "What?"

Buffy was actually enjoying this. "Ford knows I'm the Slayer."

"I know," Ford put in.

"Oh. Very good. Buffy." Giles smiled politely at Ford as he began to pull Buffy aside, saying "excuse me," to Ford. He stood a distance away with her, whispering anxiously, "You aren't by any chance betraying your secret identity just to impress ah, cute boys, are you?"

She smiled. "I didn't tell him. He knew."

"Okay. Right, then." He considered a moment. Call him Careful Man. "Just remember, if you—"

"Go," she urged him. "Experience this thing called fun. I'll try not to have a crisis."

Call it a grand tour of the metropolis by night.

Call it fifteen minutes of excruciating boredom, if you're the Slayer and used to action. Or a nice walk with a friend, if you're a sixteen-year-old girl who got unfairly expelled from her old school and exiled to this shining planet known as Sunnydale.

"And on your right, once again, the beautiful campus. I think you've now seen pretty much everything there is to see in Sunnydale."

Ford said slowly, "Well, it's really—"

"Feel free to say, 'dull.' "

"Okay." He nodded. "Dull's good." He added, "Or maybe not so dull. Is that more vampires?"

Then Buffy saw them: two vampires, sneaking toward the administration building.

She nodded. "Must be the weather."

She pulled some supplies out of her pocket: a cross for Ford and a stake for herself. To her surprise, he pulled a beginner-class stake of his own from his pocket.

"Stick close to me," she told him.

Together they snuck toward the building, up the stairs, and toward a darkened corner. Buffy scanned left, right. There were no vampires to be seen.

"Maybe they were just passing through," Ford suggested.

Buffy turned around to answer Ford. "I don't think so."

Then a blond female vampire raced up behind Buffy. Buffy punched the vamp in the forehead with her knee, then threw her into a forward roll. The girl vampire lay stunned, but a second, much bigger, vampire flung himself at Buffy and took her up and over the balcony railing.

They landed on the grass and Buffy began to whale on him: a kick to the face, a few good hard punches, and a plain, vanilla staking.

The blond lay on her back, an actual vampire. Ford bent over her with the cross, pinning her to the ground. Bizarre. Incredible.

Wonderful.

He held the stake against her chest and said in a rush, "You've got one chance to live. Tell me what I want to know, and I'll let you go."

The bigger vamp probably made a bigger dust pile. Who knew? Anyway, having an elsewhere to be,

Buffy huffed it up the stairs and found Ford, all alone.

She said, "Where's the other one?"

Ford was breathing hard, winded. "I killed her." He coughed. Coughed harder. "I killed her and she just turned to dust. It was amazing."

Buffy looked at him with new respect.

Down at the Sunset Grill . . . make that Club.

Xander, Willow, and Angel strode through the industrial section of town like the three somethings, make it Amigos, make it Stooges, make it the Kingston Trio.

Just make it more and more concerned about Buffy as Willow continued to reveal her lack of revelations.

"The only thing I could track down was this address. The Sunset Club. I still didn't find anything incriminating."

Angel stated the obvious, so at least he was good for something. "He leaves no paper trail, no records. That's incriminating enough."

"Yeah. I'm going to have to go with Dead Boy on that one," Xander said generously.

Angel was obviously irritated. "Could you not call me that?"

Zing!

They reached a particularly rundown building with a setting sun painted on a sign above the door. Angel knocked on the wide metal door. A little window slid open. Angel said, "We're friends of Ford's."

The head bobbed. The window slid shut.

The door opened.

It was some kind of underground Goth club, as spare as the Bronze, but weird and cold with blue neon lighting. Also, candles. Lots of them, in candlesticks and in candelabra. Probably a fire code violation right there. Everybody was wearing black corsets and lacy, ruffly things, and had dyed their hair ultra-black. They wore makeup that made them look as if they were all dying of tuberculosis. A fetching look. If you were Dr. Kevorkian.

As they stood on the balcony, Willow said anxiously, "Boy, we blend right in."

Xander called that and raised it a nickel. Willow had on a rainbow-colored sweater and he was in a baggy pastel shirt over a green T-shirt. "In no way do we stick out like sore thumbs."

"Let's look around," Angel said. He did not look like Happy Dead Boy, but his darker clothes blended in better. "You guys check out downstairs." He did his Angel-thing and glided away.

"Sure thing, Bossy the Cow," Xander bit off. Willow touched his arm to keep him simmering near room temperature.

The two of them started down the stairs as Angel made his way around the balcony.

Willow, as per usual, was pondering. She said, "Okay, but do they really stick out?"

Xander, as per usual, had not lifted off from the homeworld on the same trajectory. "What?"

"Sore thumbs. Do they stick out? I mean, have

you ever seen a thumb and gone, 'Wow, that baby is *sore*?"

Xander regarded her fondly. "You have too many thoughts."

From above them on the balcony, Angel checked out the scene. Xander and Willow took the last step off the metal stairs, to be greeted by a dude standing in front of a coffin.

Xander said to Willow, "Okay. Are you and I noticing a theme here?"

Willow offered, "As in 'vampires, yay'?"

"That's the one."

Speaking of yay, a Wonderbra vampirette hottie stood before them with a fetching smile of welcome on her ruby-red lips. She said, "You guys are newbies. I can tell."

"Oh, no," Willow said brightly. "We come here all the time."

Vampirella looked tolerant. "Don't be ashamed. It's cool that you're open to it. We welcome anyone who's interested in the Lonely Ones."

"The Lonely Ones?" Willow repeated.

"Vampires," Dead Boy said behind them. He was even less happy than earlier in the mission.

Xander explained to the hottie, "Oh. We usually call them the nasty pointy bitey ones."

"So many people have that misconception," the girl explained patiently. "But they who walk the night are not interested in harming anyone. They are creatures above us. Exalted."

"You're a fool." Angel's voice was so harsh that even Xander was thrown by it. Willow, too, judging by her startled expression.

The girl said, hurt, "You don't have to be so confrontational about it. Other viewpoints than yours may be valid, you know."

She drifted off, no doubt in search of those who walked the night with a more enlightened point of view. And in Xander's case at least, better clothes.

"Nice meeting you . . ." Willow called after her.

Frustrated, Xander frowned at Angel. "You're really a people person."

Willow, in her sweet way, seconded that emotion. "Now nobody's gonna talk to us."

Angel didn't let up. He was really pissed off. "I've seen enough. And I've seen this type before. They're children, making up bedtime stories about friendly vampires to comfort themselves in the dark."

Willow pondered, "Is that so bad? I mean, the dark can get pretty dark. Sometimes you need a story."

Apparently Angel wasn't feeling like giving points for good intentions. "These people don't know anything about vampires. What they are, how they live, how they dress . . ."

Just then, a guy with a ponytail sauntered by in the same reddish brown satin shirt, black pants, and black jacket as Angel's. Buffy's number-one guy actually looked embarrassed for a moment as Xander and Willow both gave him a look.

Xander observed, "You know, I love a good

diatribe, but I'm still curious why Ford, the bestest friend of the Slayer, is hanging with a bunch of vampire wannabes."

They went up the stairs, not realizing that a guy in a ruffled shirt and a sparkly blue cape, known to all who hung at the club as Diego, was listening to nearly every word they said.

Willow continued, "Something's up with him." To Angel, she offered, "You were right about that."

It was getting pretty late by the time Buffy, Giles, and Jenny Calendar swept into the library.

Buffy said, "Sorry to beep you guys in the middle of stuff, but this did seem a bit weird."

"No, you did the right thing," Giles assured her. "Absolutely."

Ms. Calendar cocked her head at him and drawled, "You hated it that much?"

"No!" he said quickly. "But vampires on campus . . . it can have implications, very grave—"

Ms. Calendar pressed, "You could have said something."

Up against the wall, British Watcher . . .

"Honestly," he said sincerely, "I've always been interested in monster trucks. I swear."

Buffy couldn't believe it. "You took him to monster trucks?"

Ms. Calendar shrugged. "I thought it would be a change."

Giles nodded. "It was a change."

"We could have just left," the techno-pagan pointed out.

"What? And miss the nitro-burning funny cars?" Giles acted very sincere. "Couldn't have that."

"Okay," Buffy interrupted, "could we get back on the vampire tip? These guys were here with a purpose."

"Yes. And we must ascertain what that purpose is," Giles agreed, settling down to business as he led the way to the study table.

"Where's your friend?" Ms. Calendar asked Buffy.

"I sent him home," Buffy replied.

"Good," Giles said. "The less he's mixed up in this, the safer he'll be."

Bragging on Ford's behalf, Buffy announced, "Well, he did bag a vamp his first time out. You gotta give him credit for that . . ." She picked something up off the table. "Who's this?"

Ms. Calendar asked, "Is something wrong?"

The photo was faded almost to a complete gray fog. The hair was different, and so was the dress, but the face that peered from it was unmistakable: it was the girl Angel had met in the playground.

"She's called Drusilla," Giles informed her. "A sometime paramour of Spike's. She was killed by an angry mob in Prague."

She was beautiful. Buffy said, "Well, they don't make angry mobs like they used to, because this girl's alive." It was humiliating, but she had to say it. "I saw her with Angel."

Giles was surprised. "With Angel?"

"Isn't he supposed to be a good guy?" Ms. Calendar asked.

The implication sank in. Deep. Buffy said quietly, "Yeah. He is."

Ms. Calender said, "I think we need to read up on this nice lady."

Giles sprang into action. He just loved this kind of stuff. "Well, some of my new volumes might be helpful." He crossed to his office as he said to Buffy and his date, "My own research has—"

Just then a blond vampire bounded out of his office with a thick old book in her hands. She pushed Giles into Buffy. They both tumbled to the floor. Then she leaped first on the table and then to the balcony, disappearing into the stacks. Buffy stared after her as Giles got up.

"You guys okay?" Ms. Calendar asked.

"A book!" Giles cried with indignation. "It took one of my books."

Ms. Calendar said wryly. "Well, at least someone in this school is reading."

More bad implications. Buffy said, half to herself, "He said he killed it." She raised her voice, looking in the direction the vampire had fled. "That's the vampire Ford said he killed."

"He lied?" Giles asked her.

He did. Buffy was adrift. "Why?"

CHAPTER 3

In their lair in an abandoned Sunnydale factory, Spike could hear Drusilla speaking in her gentle, singsong voice to her little bird in its little cage.

"You sing the sweetest little song," she cooed at it. "Won't you sing for me? Don't you love me anymore?"

Oh, criminy, not another one.

"Darling," he said in a jovial but probing voice, as he strode up to her, "I heard a funny thing just now. Lucius tells me that you went out for a hunt the other night."

She did not turn. Her eyes were on the bird.

The dead bird.

"My tummy was growly," she said. "And you were out." She focused her attention on the corpse.

"Come on." She whistled to it. "I will pout if you don't sing."

So it was true about the hunting. Had he blood pressure, it would have risen. As it was, Spike tiptoed backward into the subject. "You, uh, run into anyone? Anyone interesting?" She didn't answer. "Like Angel?"

"Angel," Drusilla said dreamily.

Spike flashed with anger. Though Angelus had brought him into this life and run with him once like a brother, he hated his sire now. But as he spoke to Drusilla, he tried to stay pleasant. "Yeah. So what might you guys have talked about, then? Old times?" His tone took on an edge. "Childhood pranks? It's a little off, you two so friendly, him being the enemy and all that . . ."

Still she ignored him. There was method to her madness; she always ignored anything she didn't want to deal with. She cocked her head at the bird and said, "I'll give you a seed if you sing."

Spike lost his patience. "The bird's dead, Dru. You left it in the cage and you didn't feed it and now it's all dead. Just like the last one."

She whimpered, a high, little-girl-lost keening she made whenever she was unhappy and might cry. At once he softened. It was not her fault she was insane.

"I'm sorry, baby. I'm a bad, rude man. I just don't like you going out, that's all. You are weak." He picked up her hand and sucked on one of her fingers. "Would you like a new bird? One that's not dead?"

And she smiled. Up at him. Not up at Angel, or some foggy memory of love lost. At Spike.

The moment was shattered by the callow cry of a young human, exclaiming, "This is so cool! I could really live here."

Spike spun in its direction, murder on his true, vampiric face. The speaker was a boy who slightly resembled the friend of the Slayer, the mouthy one called Xander.

"Do I have anyone on watch here?" Spike bellowed, furious. "It's called security, people. Are you all asleep?"

He crossed to the boy and smiled. "Or did we finally find a restaurant that delivers."

Now Spike's people began to emerge. One here, one there, moving from the shadows. The kid stood his ground. Spike had to give him that. It was clear he was nervous—and just as clear that he was getting a rush from his fear. Spike had known many humans like that.

Briefly.

"I know who you are," the boy announced.

Spike retorted testily, "I know who I am, too. So what?"

"I came here looking for you." So boyish. So eager. So about to be dead. "You are Spike, right? William the Bloody?"

"You've got a real death wish." One of Spike's minions, a blond vampire named Julia, approached and handed him a book. She looked startled to see the boy. Spike would have to find out why later. "It's almost interesting."

Spike opened the book and leafed through it, pleased. It had all kinds of Slayer lore in it.

"Oh, this is great," he said happily. "This will be very useful." He kept paging through it, not deigning to look at the boy. "So, how'd you find me?"

The boy said, "That doesn't matter. I've got something to offer you." Spike looked up. "I'm pretty sure this is the part where you take out a watch and say I've got thirty seconds to convince you not to kill me," the child continued. "It's traditional."

Who did this little pipsqueak think he was? "Well." Spike slammed the book shut and threw it on the ground. "I don't much go for tradition."

He flew at the boy and grabbed his ear. The boy's eyes widened with fear and he began to pant. Good. It would make his blood so much richer. . . .

Drusilla put her hand on Spike's shoulder and said, "Wait, love."

She had that tone she got when she saw things: call 'em visions, whatever. He had learned to trust her instincts. If not her pet-care habits.

"Well?" Spike demanded of the boy.

"Come on. Say it. It's no fun if you don't say it."

Spike growled, "What? Oh." He rolled his eyes. With absolutely no enthusiasm, he ran down the litany. "You've got thirty seconds to convince me not to kill you."

The boy was thrilled. "Yes! See? This is the best!" He came down a little, but he was still beaming like a traffic light. "I want to be like you. A vampire."

Spike was amused. A little disappointed that it wasn't something more bizarre, but amused. "I've known you for two minutes and I can't stand you. I don't really feature you living forever." To Dru, he said, "Can I eat him now, love?"

"Well, feature this," the boy continued, undaunted. "I'm offering a trade. You make me a vampire. And I give you the Slayer."

Spike had to admit the boy had his attention now. He had everyone's attention.

Buffy's mom had another late night at the gallery. Buffy was home alone, making cocoa, when Angel appeared at her kitchen door. He said, "Buffy. May I come in?"

Buffy took a moment to compose herself and said, "Sure. I thought once you'd been invited you could always just walk in."

"I can," he replied, walking into the kitchen. "I was being polite." She put her hands around her warm cup. She felt cold, down her heart.

He continued, in a serious, urgent voice. "We need to talk."

She swallowed. "Do we." She picked up her cup and headed for the dining room. It wasn't really a question. She wanted to ask him, *Don't you love me anymore? How can you lie to me about another girl after all we've gone through together?* But she kept those questions to herself.

He followed her into the room. "It's about your friend, Ford," he said. "He's not what he seems."

She looked up at him, at the dark eyes and the mouth that was always sad, even when Angel smiled.

It occurred to her that she had never heard him laugh.

"Who is these days?" she asked shortly.

Angel was missing, or ignoring, her jibes. "Willow ran him down on the computer."

"Willow?" She was stung. Willow had invaded an old friend's privacy and not even bothered to tell her?

"We found this address. We checked it out with Xander and it turned out to—"

"And Xander?" Buffy echoed. "Wow, everybody's in. It's a great big, exciting conspiracy." She sat down.

Angel paused. "What are you talking about?"

"I'm talking about the people I trust." She looked up at him, looked at him hard. "Who's Drusilla?" Angel's face fell as if she had told him of the death of someone close. Though shaken, she refused to give up now. "And don't lie to me. I'm tired of it."

He looked tired, weary, and very sad. "Some lies are necessary."

"For what?" she demanded.

"Sometimes the truth is worse." He gazed away, then back at her. "You live long enough, you find that out."

"I can take it. I can take the truth."

"Do you love me?" he asked, searching her face.

She was startled. "What?"

"Do you?"

And here it was, the question lovers always ask each other, ask themselves. The Slayer's vampire boyfriend, asking it of her. Had she not asked herself the same question over and over, trying to make sense of it?

Her eyes welled. "I love you," she admitted. "I don't know if I can trust you."

"Maybe you shouldn't do either."

"Maybe I'm the one who should decide," she answered defiantly.

He waited a beat. Then, as if what he would say next would cost him dearly, he began.

It came out in a rush, as if he wanted it over and done.

"I did a lot of unconscionable things when I became a vampire. Drusilla was the worst. She was an . . . obsession of mine. She was pure and sweet and chaste."

"You made her a vampire," Buffy said slowly, as the awful truth dawned.

"First I made her insane. Killed everyone she loved, visited every mental torture on her I could devise. She eventually fled to a convent and the day she took her holy orders I turned her into a demon."

For a moment Buffy couldn't say a word. She couldn't even look at him.

"Well, I asked for the truth," she said slowly, wondering how to heal after knowing this of him. Wondering if she could still love him.

But Angel looked for no forgiveness. His thoughts were only of Buffy's safety. "Ford's part of some society that reveres vampires. Practically worships them. I don't know what he wants from you. But you can't trust him."

The next day at school Buffy's thoughts were crowded with all the things Angel had told her the night before.

"Buffy!" Ford cried.

Including the fact that she couldn't trust an old friend.

"Ford," she said, and tried to smile. His own smile seemed predatory, calculated.

"I had a great time last night," he told her. Then he chuckled and said, "Well, an interesting one."

Masking her feelings, Buffy replied, "I'm glad."

"Do you want to go out again tonight?"

She made herself smile. "I'm not busy."

"I sort of had an idea. It's a secret. I kind of want to surprise you."

"I like surprises." What Slayer didn't?

"Can you meet me here?" he asked.

"Sure."

He was pleased. "At nine?"

"At nine."

He bent and whispered in her ear, "It's going to be fun."

Xander and Willow were sitting morosely on the stairway, reminding Buffy of the many times she herself had been sent to the principal's office.

Willow said anxiously, "Hey, Buffy. Did, uh, Angel—"

"He told me everything," Buffy could hear the chilliness in her own voice, and wished it wasn't there. Wished there was no reason for it be there.

Willow went on, "I'm sorry we kept stuff from you."

"It's okay," Buffy told her. She almost meant it.

"When Angel came to my room he was just really concerned for you," Willow told her. "And we didn't want to say anything in case we were wrong."

Dear Willow. Buffy could never stay angry at her. She put her hand on Willow's arm.

Xander said, "Did you find out what Ford is up to?"

"I will," Buffy replied. She left.

They watched her go. After a moment Xander registered what Willow had said and stared at Willow in shock.

"Angel was in your *bedroom?*"

Willow looked pensive. "Ours is a forbidden love."

And here they were, the True Believers. What did Ford make, the thirteenth guest? He went down the stairs of the Sunset Club.

"Chantarelle," he said to the lovely blond clad all in scarlet and jet. She wore a large red choker with a big hunk of red glass in the center. "Is everything ready?"

The nerd formerly known as Marvin bustled up and said, irritated, "Of course it's ready. Hi. I took care of it. I always take care of it."

Chantarelle's eyes lit up. She said, with awe in her voice, "Is it time? Tonight?"

Ford asked her, "Are you nervous?"

"Yes," she admitted. "No." She straightened her shoulders. "I'm ready for the change. Do you really think they'll bless us?"

"I know they will," Ford told her proudly. "Everything's falling into place."

Diego cut in. "What about your friends? Are they coming?"

Ford blinked. "What are you talking about?"

"Your friends," Diego filled in. "They came last night. Two guys and a girl."

Chantarelle added, "One was mean."

Ford's stomach did a flip. "Why didn't you tell me about this?"

Diego was irritated and defensive. "I have to do everything around here. Sorry, Mr. Flawless Plan Guy. It slipped my mind."

Chantarelle frowned. "It's going to be all right, isn't it? They're not going to let us down?"

Ford didn't have time for this. "It's going to be fine."

She persisted, "I need them to bless me."

Exasperated, Ford repeated, "It's going to be *fine.*"

"No. It's really not," said a voice.

Ford turned. Buffy was coming down the steps.

Ford's face hardened. He glanced at Diego, and murmured, "It's kind of drafty in here."

Diego sidled off as Buffy drew near.

* * *

Buffy knew she had to keep her wits about her, but she was hurt and angry as she stopped on the stairs to look down on Ford. Still, she hid it all inside. She had gotten very good at that.

"I'm sorry, Ford," she said airily, moving down again. "I just couldn't wait until tonight. I'm rash and impulsive. It's a flaw."

Ford shrugged. "We all have flaws."

"I'm still fuzzy on exactly what yours is." She reached the floor and faced her old friend. "I think it has to do with being a lying scumbag."

"Everybody lies."

"What do you want, Ford? What's this all about?" she asked.

"I really don't think you'd understand."

"I don't need to understand. I just need to know." And she was not requesting information; she was demanding it.

He said, "I'm going to be one of them."

She digested that. "You want to be a vampire."

"I'm going to," he said.

"Vampires are kind of picky about who they change." And then it hit her: "You were going to offer them a trade." She was shocked beyond words. Her old friend had been planning her death.

Ford said, "I don't think I want to talk anymore."

Buffy grabbed him and slammed him up against the wall, hand against his throat. "Well, I still feel awfully chatty. You were going to give them me. Tonight."

"Yes," he said gruffly, his vocal cords constricted by her grip.

"You had to know I'd figure it out, Ford."

Ford smiled. "Actually, I was counting on it." He started laughing, then coughing, then wheezing as he grinned at her.

She stepped back, wary, and let him go. He kept laughing and coughing. It gave her a wiggins. "What's supposed to happen tonight?"

"This is so cool! This is just like it played in my head. The part where you ask me what's supposed to happen—it's already happening."

The big door slammed shut. Immediately Buffy raced up the stairs to it and pulled. She couldn't open it. There was no doorknob and no other way to open it.

She turned around to face Ford. He was halfway up the stairs, the others grouped around him like some macabre class picture.

"Rigged it up special," he told her. "Once it's closed, it can only be opened from the outside. As soon as the sun sets, they'll be coming."

Buffy appealed to him. "Ford, if these people are still around when they get here—"

The guy in the blue cape said, "We'll be changed, all of us."

"We're going to ascend to a new level of consciousness," the blond bimbo, Chantarelle, explained. "Become like them, like the Lonely Ones."

"This is the end, Buffy." Ford's face was set, determined, his smile a mask. "No one gets out of here alive."

Buffy raced down the stairs, looking for an alternate exit. Ford was on her heels.

She said, "There's gotta be a way out of here."

"This is a bomb shelter, Buffy," Ford told her as she pulled back a black velvet curtain and found a bricked-in doorway. "I knew I wasn't going to be able to overpower you. But this is three feet of solid concrete. Trust me when I say we're here for the long haul."

"At least let the other people go," Buffy said.

"Why are you fighting this?" Chantarelle asked her. "It's what we want."

"It's our chance for immortality," Cape Guy added.

"This is a beautiful day!" Chantarelle went on. "Can't you see that?"

Buffy shot back, "What I can see is that right after the sun goes down, Spike and all of his friends are going to be pigging out at the all-you-can-eat moron bar."

Cape Guy said, "Okay. That's it. I think we should gag her."

Buffy gave him a look possessed only by Slayers. "I think you should try."

Cape Guy persisted, "She's an unbeliever. She taints us."

"I am trying to save you," Buffy insisted. "You're playing in some serious traffic here, do you understand that? You're going to *die*. And the only hope you have of surviving is to get out of this pit right now and, my God, could you *have* a dorkier outfit?"

Cape Guy looked hurt.

Ford smiled. "I've got to back her up, D. You look like a big ninny."

A little alarm went off. Ford dug into his pocket and pulled out a pager. He smiled triumphantly.

"Six twenty-seven," he announced. "Sunset."

Sunset.

As Spike's people assembled for the hunt, he called out his instructions. "When we get there, everybody spread out. Two men on the door. First priority is the Slayer. Everything else is fair game, but let's remember to *share,* people."

He went over to Dru. "Are you sure you're up for this?"

"I want a treat," she said, her head lolling. "I need a treat."

"And a special one you'll have." He gathered up her hair and smiled into her beautiful face. Their bloodlust rose in one rhythm. It was astonishing how much he loved this girl.

"Lucius!" Spike held up a set of keys. "Bring the car around."

Buffy was still trying to find a way out. She raced back up the stairs and felt around the knobless door.

Ford said, "Man, you never give up, do you?"

"No, I don't," Buffy replied.

"That's a good quality in a person. Too many people, they just lay back and take it. But us—"

"Us? We have something in common now?" She walked around the balcony. Ford followed her.

"More than you'd think," Ford told her.

"Okay, let me explain something to you," Buffy

said, whirling on him. "You're what we call the bad guy."

"I guess I am," he said, as if he hadn't thought of that before, but he liked it nonetheless.

She looked down at his friends in their ruffles and black lipstick, milling around and wondering what was going to happen next. "These people aren't going to get changed, are they? The rest of them, they're just fodder."

"Technically, yes. But I'm in. I will become immortal." He wasn't even ashamed to say it.

She flared. "I've got a newsflash for you, braintrust. That's not how it works. You die. And a demon sets up shop in your old house. And it walks and talks and remembers your life, but it's not you."

He looked away for a moment, then back at her. "It's better than nothing," Ford said.

Buffy was shocked. "And your life is nothing?" He laughed bitterly. "Ford, these people don't deserve to die."

"Neither do I!" he flung at her. His voice broke. "But apparently nobody took that into consideration, because I'm still dying."

She blinked.

"I look good, don't I? Let me tell you something. I've got maybe six months left and by then what they bury won't even look like me. It'll be bald and shriveled and it'll smell bad. I'm not going out that way."

She turned away.

"I'm sorry, Summers. Did I screw up your righteous anger riff? Does the nest of tumors liquefying my brain kind of spoil the fun?"

"I'm sorry." She faced him again, with tears of pity in her eyes. "I had no idea. But what you're doing is still very wrong."

"Okay, well, you try vomiting for twenty-four hours straight because the pain in your head is so intense and then we'll discuss the concept of right and wrong." He gestured toward the others. "These people are sheep. They want to be vampires because they're lonely, or miserable, or bored. I don't have a choice."

"You have a choice. You *don't* have a good choice, but you have a choice. You're opting for mass murder here and nothing you say to me is going to make that okay."

Ford said, "Do you think I need to justify myself to you?"

Buffy answered, "I think this is all part of your little fantasy drama. Isn't this exactly how you imagined it? You tell me how you've suffered and I feel sorry for you. Well, I do feel sorry for you, and if those vampires come in here and start feeding, I'll kill you myself."

For a moment the ghost of a smile passed over his face, and he was the old Ford again, the manly sixth grader she had moped over for months. He said quietly, "You know what, Summers? I really did miss you."

A car engine hummed. Tires squealed. They were here.

Maybe there was enough of the old Ford still there, she hoped. Just as Angel's soul had been restored, maybe she could appeal to what had been Ford before his illness had changed him. She said, "Ford, help me stop this. *Please.*"

But she saw that the moment was over. He was determined to carry out his plan.

She headed around the balcony and started down the stairs.

"People, listen to me," Buffy pleaded. "This is not the mothership, okay? This is ugly death come to play."

Ford hit her, hard, with a crowbar. Buffy clattered down the stairs. She rose, turned, and tried to defend herself as Ford hit her again, sending her sliding.

Chantarelle had not expected violence, and it frightened her. This was not the way she thought it would happen. Yet the Lonely Ones were poised to enter, and so she prepared herself. Slowly she walked up the stairs.

The door swung open. A figure with a horrible face and a shock of white hair stepped in. Others trooped in behind him.

He snarled at her and ripped off her red choker. She was terrified of him.

The vampire said, "Take them all. Save the Slayer for me!"

As he buried his fangs in her neck, the other vampires charged down the steps and began grabbing Chantarelle's friends. They savagely bit into their necks, feasting.

They were not exalted. This was not a sacred moment. It was a lie. A terrible lie . . .

Ford came around the couch with the crowbar. Coming to, Buffy grabbed the bar, wrenched it free, and slammed Ford headfirst into a pillar. He fell to the floor.

And then Buffy saw the girl.

Spike's girl.

Angel's girl.

Drusilla was standing on the balcony, looking dazed and hungry. Without hesitation, Buffy ran and, pushing off the sofa, jumped onto the balcony. She landed next to Drusilla and grabbed her, whipped out a stake, and placed it directly over the cold, mad girl's heart.

"Spike!" Drusilla cried.

Spike froze. He looked genuinely frightened. He immediately released Chantarelle, who slumped and burst into tears.

"Everybody *stop!*" Spike yelled.

Everyone did.

"Good idea," Buffy said, keeping the stake firmly pressed against Drusilla's chest. "Now you let everybody out or your girlfriend fits in an ashtray."

"Spike?" Drusilla called anxiously.

"It's going to be all right, baby." He said to his people, "Let them go."

The True Believers flew out of the open door of

the Sunset Club like bats out of hell. Cape Guy pushed his way to the front. The last of them stopped to help Chantarelle.

Buffy started toward the door keeping Drusilla close. At the last minute she hurled her down at Spike. Spike caught his baby as Buffy got to the door and stepped out, slamming it shut behind her.

Spike raced up to the closed door with his men. He looked at it and paused.

"Uh, where's the doorknob?" he asked.

Buffy stepped out to find the True Believers escaping into the night. Xander, Willow, and Angel had converged just outside the Sunset Club.

Buffy said, "You guys got here just in time."

Willow piped up. "Are there vampires—"

Buffy nodded. "They're contained. They'll get out eventually, though. We should clear out. We can come back when they're gone."

Xander said, "Come back for what?"

Buffy felt anger again, laid over with a deep, heavy sorrow. "For the body," she answered.

He was still alive.

Ford stood up groggily and took in his surroundings. His head hurt terribly. He said, "What happened?"

Spike answered hotly, "We're stuck in the basement."

Ford looked around. "Buffy?"

The vampire retorted, "She's *not* stuck in the basement."

Ford gave him a shrug that said it all. *You win some. You lose some.* "Hey, well, I delivered. I handed her to you."

"Yes, I suppose you did," the vampire answered him.

Ford said, "So what about my reward?"

Spike and Drusilla stared at him.

Hungrily.

Buffy returned by daylight to the find the scene exactly as she had imagined it: the special door partially ripped off at its hinges.

On the stairs, Ford lay outstretched, his dead eyes staring.

EPILOGUE

In the graveyard, Giles stood by as Buffy placed roses on the fresh grave of Billy Fordham. Moonlight wafted wanly through the trees where so many dramas had played out in Buffy's life. It was here that Angel and she had bickered about going on a date. In a nearby crypt, she had asked him, joking, if he knew what it was like to have a friend.

And now she was burying someone who had once been a friend.

She looked up at Giles. "I don't know what I'm supposed to say."

"You needn't say anything," he replied kindly.

"It'd be simpler if I could just hate him. I think he

wanted me to. I think it made it easier for him to be the villain of the piece. Really, he was just scared."

"Yes, I suppose he was," Giles offered.

"Nothing's ever simple anymore. I'm constantly trying to work it out. Who to love, or hate . . . who to trust. It's just, like the more I know, the more confused I get."

Giles's smile was brief and sad. "I believe that's called growing up."

In a little voice, she answered, "I'd like to stop then, okay?"

"I know the feeling." His smile spoke of memories he had not yet shared.

"Well, does it ever get easy?" she asked.

Suddenly Ford burst from his grave, not Ford at all, but a snarling vampire covered with graveyard dirt. Mindlessly, he lunged at them. With one swift strike, Buffy drove a stake into his chest and he exploded into dust. Immortality denied.

"You mean life?" Giles asked her.

"Yeah," Buffy said. "Does it get easy?"

Giles looked puzzled. "What do you want me to say?"

She thought about it a moment. Then she pleaded gently, "Lie to me."

Giles took on a bright, teacherly tone. "Yes. It's terribly simple."

They started out of the graveyard.

"The good guys are stalwart and true. The bad guys are easily distinguished by their pointy horns or black hats and we always defeat them and save the day. No one ever dies, and everybody lives happily ever after."

And Buffy assessed the truth of what he said with one simple word: "Liar."

THE CHRONICLES:

EPILOGUE

"**N**obody ever dies, and everyone lives happily ever after."

Angel watched from the shadows as Slayer and Watcher walked from the graveyard. Her friend, Ford, was dead. Drusilla still lived.

Both he and Buffy had died—she had drowned at the hands of the Master, and Xander had brought her back. And he, Angel, had died when he was made a vampire, and died again—inside—when his soul was restored and he regained the ability to feel remorse . . . as well as to love someone genuinely and utterly.

Now she and he together stumbled along, learning about each other, confessing, revealing, daring.

Would he and Buffy live happily ever after? He had no idea. He only knew that his truth was this: he loved her, and he was mortally sorry, to the depths of his being, that there was so much about him that was unlovable.

He stayed in the shadows as the moon glowed on Buffy's golden hair.

He stayed there until minutes before the dawn.

ABOUT THE AUTHOR

Four-time Bram Stoker Award winner Nancy Holder has sold forty novels and over two hundred short stories, articles, and essays. Her work has appeared on the *Los Angeles Times, USA Today,* and Amazon.com bestseller lists. Alone and with her frequent collaborator, Christopher Golden, she has written a dozen *Buffy the Vampire Slayer* projects, including *The Watcher's Guide* and *Immortal,* the first *Buffy* hardcover novel, due out for Halloween 1999. She has also written several short stories with Golden, and appears in two of the anthologies he edited, including the award-winning *CUT!: Horror Writers on Horror Film.*

Holder's work has been translated into two dozen languages, and she has also written comic books, game fiction, and television commercials. She is currently completing the last volume of a science fiction trilogy called *Gambler's Star* for Avon Books.

A graduate of the University of California at San Diego, she lives in San Diego with her husband, Wayne, and their daughter, Belle.

SPIKE AND DRU:
PRETTY MAIDS ALL IN A ROW

The year is 1940.

In exchange for a powerful jewel, Spike and Drusilla
agree to kill the current Slayer—and all those targeted
to succeed her. If they succeed with their plans of
bloodlust and power, it could mean the end of the
Chosen One—*all* of the Chosen Ones—forever....

A *Buffy* hardcover
by Christopher Golden

Available from Pocket Books

Everyone's got his demons....

ANGEL™

If it takes an eternity, he will make amends.

❖

Original stories based on the
TV show created by Joss Whedon
& David Greenwalt

Available from Pocket Pulse
Published by Pocket Books

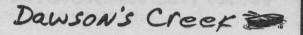

Dawson's Creek

**Look for more new,
original Dawson's Creek™ stories
wherever books are sold.**

And don't miss:

Dawson's Creek
The Official Postcard Book

Dawson's Creek
The Official Scrapbook

Available now from Pocket Pulse
Published by Pocket Books

**Visit Pocket Books on the World Wide Web
http://www.SimonSays.com**

**Visit the Sony website at
*http://www.dawsonscreek.com***

"Wish me monsters."

—Buffy, "Living Conditions"

Vampires, werewolves, witches, demons of nonspecific origin...

They're all here in this extensive guide to the monsters of *Buffy* and their mythological, literary, and cultural origins.

Includes interviews with the show's writers and creator Joss Whedon

THE MONSTER BOOK

By
Christopher Golden
(co-author of THE WATCHER'S GUIDE)
Stephen R. Bissette
Thomas E. Sniegoski

FROM

POCKET BOOKS